100 Reasons to Celebrate

We invite you to join us in celebrating
Mills & Boon's centenary. Gerald Mills and
Charles Boon founded Mills & Boon Limited
in 1908 and opened offices in London's Covent
Garden. Since then, Mills & Boon has become
a hallmark for romantic fiction, recognised
around the world.

We're proud of our 100 years of publishing
excellence, which wouldn't have been achieved
without the loyalty and enthusiasm of our
authors and readers.

Thank you!

Each month throughout the year there will
be something new and exciting to mark the
centenary, so watch for your favourite authors,
captivating new stories, special limited
edition collections…and more!

Dear Reader

HER VERY SPECIAL BABY was such a joy to write. The seaside town isn't too far from where we live, and it is full of such wonderful history—from the horse-drawn tram which initially began in 1894, to the hundred-year-old Town Hall which is still in use today. Although this little town isn't as old as other amazing places in the world, its richness is personal to those who live there and in surrounding districts. History has the ability to set us up for who we can become, and to help us look forward into the future with determination and promise.

This year Mills & Boon is also turning one hundred, and it all began with the determination and promise of two men—Gerald Mills and Charles Boon—who wanted to start their own publishing company. A century later we are proud to be a part of its continuing success.

Being able to write engaging romantic stories for Mills & Boon is definitely a dream come true. Granted, it can be a challenge to find the right combination of ingredients—to find the mix of characters, emotional tension, internal conflict and that obligatory serving of love each story needs. But we know with determination and promise—combined with a lot of hard work—an inspirational story of encouragement and romance will always be created. Bringing joy to readers, receiving positive feedback and loving what we do makes our job the best in the world.

With warmest centenary regards

Lucy Clark

HER VERY
SPECIAL BABY

BY
LUCY CLARK

MILLS & BOON®

Pure reading pleasure

All the characters in this book have no existence outside the imagination of the author, and have no relation whatsoever to anyone bearing the same name or names. They are not even distantly inspired by any individual known or unknown to the author, and all the incidents are pure invention.

First published in Great Britain 2007
Harlequin Mills & Boon Limited,
Eton House, 18-24 Paradise Road, Richmond, Surrey TW9 1SR

© Anne Clark and Peter Clark 2007

ISBN: 978 0 263 86305 5

Set in Times Roman 10½ on 12¼ pt
03-0208-52111

Printed and bound in Spain
by Litografia Rosés, S.A., Barcelona

Lucy Clark is actually a husband-and-wife writing team. They enjoy taking holidays with their children, during which they discuss and develop new ideas for their books using the fantastic Australian scenery. They use their daily walks to talk over characterisation and fine details of the wonderful stories they produce, and are avid movie buffs. They live on the edge of a popular wine district in South Australia with their two children, and enjoy spending family time together at weekends.

Recent titles by the same author:

HIS CHRISTMAS PROPOSAL
THE EMERGENCY DOCTOR'S DAUGHTER
THE SURGEON'S COURAGEOUS BRIDE
IN HIS SPECIAL CARE
A KNIGHT TO HOLD ON TO

For John. Thanks, bro.
James 3:17

CHAPTER ONE

'I HATE being late.' Morena parked her car and headed for the general practice she'd inherited from her father. 'Half an hour late for morning clinic,' she muttered as she looked at her watch, wishing it was lying to her, but she knew it kept perfect time. 'It's not going to be a good day.' Pasting on a smile, expecting the waiting room to be full, she entered the clinic.

'Good morning, Morena.' Sally greeted her from behind the orange laminated reception counter. In all the years Morena had come here, first as a child to visit her father then as a teenager to help with the clerical work then as an employee and now as the boss, the bright and cheery atmosphere never failed to lift her spirits—late or not. Today, however, things were different.

'Sorry I'm late. Connor just wouldn't settle properly for Mum.'

'Not a problem. We're running ahead of schedule.'

'Oh.' That wasn't what Morena had expected. 'New locum's first day on the job and we're ahead of schedule. A good beginning for him. A not-so-positive impression for me.' Morena rolled her eyes and turned her attention from the blonde receptionist when the sound of the spare consulting-room door opened. Mrs Henderson came out of the room and she was *smiling*. Mrs Henderson never smiled at *anyone* and she was also chatting away like a sparrow.

'My favourites are ANZAC biscuits, especially when they're a little soft.' The deep masculine voice floated towards them all and Morena felt rather than saw the two women in the waiting room sigh. Goose bumps raged up and down Morena's back and she quickly told herself it was because today was the locum's first day and she'd wanted to make a good impression—which she'd obviously failed at by being so late. Of course, it had nothing to do with his smooth-as-silk voice.

'Well, my dear boy,' Mrs Henderson was saying as she fluttered her eyelashes at him. 'I must bring you my special ANZAC biscuits.' She leaned closer and touched his arm. 'I put double the golden syrup in and that's what makes them taste better than anyone else's.'

'I look forward to it, Mrs Henderson.' As he spoke, the man in question came into view. It was strange, seeing someone else here in her father's practice, but she had to admit Dr Nathan Young, who had applied for the job displaying excellent qualifications, looked good in the outdated décor of Victor Harbor's family practice.

He was tall, about six feet four inches, with dark brown hair and deep, *deep* brown eyes. This fact she registered as their gazes met. Time seemed to stand still for those few seconds, so much so that Morena was able to see the flecks of gold that sparked out from the pupil and the vibrant chocolate brown of the halo outlining the iris. As he turned his attention back to Mrs Henderson, Morena breathed in and was treated to subtle spicy scent which enveloped her. She liked it.

Shaking her head as though to clear it from the daze he'd evoked, she forced a smile as Mrs Henderson made her way fully into the waiting room. The woman, who considered herself almost like royalty in these parts, given the fact that her husband had been mayor for many years until his retirement, looked down her nose at Morena.

'Dr Camden.' The dour and insolent glare was back as she breezed past her. 'I must say I'm pleased to see this practice finally employing someone with breeding, stature and is, above all, a true professional.' Her lips twitched a little as her eyes looked over Dr Young once more.

Morena was more than used to Mrs Henderson's opinion of the practice. 'Yes. Thank you. I'm glad you approve.'

'What's not to approve of? Dr Young has been…delightful.'

Morena glanced at Dr Young and saw him incline his head in a slight bow. 'It was my pleasure, Mrs Henderson. Feel free to call me at any time if you need any further medical advice or assistance.'

'There you are. Perfect breeding.' Mrs Henderson made a grand sweeping gesture with her hand, indicating the two ladies who were sitting breathlessly ogling Dr Young. 'Make your appointments with Dr Young if you require more than the basic care.'

Morena tried hard not to roll her eyes and give the old battleaxe a piece of her mind. All she had to do was control her temper for a few more minutes and then Mrs Henderson would leave—hopefully without comment on Morena's personal situation.

'Do you require another appointment, Mrs Henderson?' Sally asked.

'Dr Camden,' Mrs Henderson said, ignoring the receptionist. 'I see you're running a little behind time this morning. Not at all the way this clinic should be run.'

'Yes, Mrs Henderson.'

'I trust Connor is in good health?'

'Perfect health. And your husband? How has he been feeling?'

'Staid as Granite Island as always, Dr Camden. My Hoban has never had a day of sickness in his life. Even in retirement, he is always up early and out of doors, enjoying himself in the community.'

'Of course. Please, pass on my warmest regards to Mr Henderson.'

All she received was a look of disdain and a cold shoulder. Clenching her jaw and working extremely hard at controlling her temper, Morena could feel herself about to bubble over.

'Dr Camden? If you're free for a moment, I have some questions.' Dr Young indicated his consulting-room door. Morena looked at him again and when he angled his head slightly she seemed to snap out of whatever bond was holding her.

'Right. Of course. Have a nice day, Mrs Henderson.' With that, Morena walked on, her bag still slung over her shoulder, into the assigned consulting room of Dr Young. She heard him make his farewells to the woman no one had ever been able to raise a smile from, and within another moment he was in the room with the door shut behind them.

'Whew! That was close.' He smiled at her and she felt her knees weaken. His teeth were white, his eyes were twinkling and she was certain he was laughing at her. Clutching the desk for support, she turned away from him and ordered herself to start behaving.

'What was close?'

'You—about to lose your temper with Mrs H.'

'Mrs H.? Don't let her hear you calling her that. She'll have your head.' Morena turned around as she spoke and watched as he looked at her inquisitively, his eyebrows raised.

'Do you really think so?'

'Hmm, probably not. You seem to have her wrapped around you little finger. I'm Morena, by the way.' She held out her hand and her bag slipped down to her elbow. 'Oops.' It didn't seem to matter because the instant he placed his warm hand in hers she forgot everything around her and once more found herself becoming lost in those rich, chocolaty depths.

His smile was still dazzling her and she was sure he'd be perfect for a toothpaste advertisement, so natural was his appeal. The sounds outside the small room drifted away, leaving just the two of them, standing there, holding hands for longer than was required in a professional introduction such as this.

'Nathan.' He didn't seem in any hurry to let her hand go and the realisation made her wonder about her own appearance. She hadn't had time to check it before rushing out the door at the first available opportunity. Was her hair a mess? Did she have lipstick smeared on her teeth? She wouldn't be surprised, given that she'd whacked her lipstick on while driving.

'You weren't able to make it to my interview,' Nathan was saying, bringing her thoughts back to the present. He released her hand and as she let go, her bag slid from her arm and dropped to the floor. Quickly, and with a little nervous laugh, Morena hoisted it back onto her shoulder.

'No. I wasn't, but I trust my father's judgement. He was, after all, choosing his replacement.'

'Replacement? I understood he would still be practising part time.'

'Two half-days per week and the odd emergency—if you or I are unavailable. If I had my way, he'd be retiring completely.'

'You want him out of the picture so you can do things your way?' Odd. She hadn't struck him as that type of person. 'Out with the old, in with the new?'

'No!' She seemed appalled. 'Heavens, no. Not at all. I'd love it if he could stay on and work here for ever, but it's his health. He has angina and the stress of running a busy family practice isn't good for him. Mum's been trying to get him to slow down for years but even after we started working here, things seemed to increase, rather than the opposite.'

'We? I didn't know your mother was a doctor.'

'Hmm?' Morena was confused. 'She's not.'

'But you said *we*.'

'Oh. Sorry. I keep forgetting you're not from around here and therefore don't know every ounce of gossip, although I'm sure you'll hear more than enough in the course of the morning. No, the "we" I was referring to was my husband and I.'

Nathan's eyes flicked to her left hand but there was no ring there—although he could make out a very faint tan line.

'I'm divorced now,' she added quickly, wondering why she was so eager to impart that bit of information. She watched him closely but no new emotion crossed his face.

'I take it all the patients gossip about it?'

Morena laughed without humour. 'I think you'll hardly be able to avoid it, although it's not such an interesting story when all is said and done.'

'Why don't you give me your side first, then?'

'What? And spoil any fun you may get from being told the story over and over ad nauseam? Perish the thought, Dr Young.'

'Spoilsport.'

She chuckled. 'I've been called that more than once.'

Nathan's smile was still there, his eyes twinkling at her, making her feel happy and smart—and she wanted it to continue. This easy, friendly banter, the way he looked at her, made her feel. Her eyes widened with the realisation that she'd been flirting with him. Flirting with her new colleague!

Clearing her throat, she forced herself to look away and shifted the bag on her shoulder. 'Anyway, you said you had some questions?'

'Not really. I just said that to get you away from Mrs H. Victor

Harbor seems like a nice place.' He barely paused for breath before continuing, 'Did you really kick your husband out?'

'Pardon?'

'Mrs H. said you did the right thing by getting rid of him. She called him a wandering philanderer.'

Morena found it impossible to keep her smile in place but she found it even harder to ignore the pang of failure that came every time someone mentioned her disastrous marriage. 'I see your fun has already begun. How nice of Mrs Henderson to give her opinion.' She looked down at her hands and forced herself to breathe.

'It does bother you, then,' he stated. 'It's not too late to give me your version.'

She was silent for a moment, the ticking of the clock on the wall the only sound in the room. Shrugging, she decided she may as well. What harm could it do? 'I married the wrong man. Simple as that. I've learnt a lot about life as well as myself along the way and *should* there ever be a next time, I'll be doing things very differently.'

'How so?'

'We don't really have the time to go into it now and it's all water over the bridge...or is it under the bridge? I always get that saying confused. Anyway, the tide has turned, the water has changed and that's that.'

'Hmm.' He nodded, a very thoughtful expression on his face. 'I'm sorry if I've upset you, Morena.'

'No. It's fine.' She waved his words away but was secretly touched at the sincerity in his eyes.

'It's quite common, you know.'

'Divorce? Yes, I know.'

'No. I meant it's common to be sensitive where affairs of the heart are concerned.'

'Oh.' That surprised her and it also made her realise that

Nathan obviously had experience with emotional heart problems. It was on the tip of her tongue to ask him what had happened in his life when she saw his expression change. It was as though he'd physically slipped a mask into place, warning her off. She also wondered if he'd regretted saying too much to a woman who was a relative stranger.

'I didn't mean to pry. Forgive me?'

She was taken aback at that, wondering if any man had ever asked her for forgiveness before. She was also desperate to get back to the easy banter they'd enjoyed a few minutes ago. That had been nice. Forcing a smile, she nodded slowly. 'I guess I'm going to have to…but only this once, you understand. Don't go making a habit out of it.'

'Out of what? Asking for forgiveness?'

She'd expected him to smile at her words, to realise she was teasing, to join in her attempt to lighten the atmosphere a little.

Instead, he was quite stern as he said very softly, 'I doubt I'll ever stop.' And there it was. For a fraction of a second, the mask slipped and she saw the pain, the anguish, the emptiness behind his eyes. It was clear he'd known true pain, true heartbreak and true bleakness.

The intercom on the desk buzzed and Morena, slightly startled, spun around to look at it as Sally's voice came through. 'Morena? You still in there? Nathan? Can I send your next patient through?'

'Work,' Morena stated, as Nathan came around the desk.

'Work,' he echoed, as he pressed the button and told Sally to send his next patient through.

Morena glanced at him again before leaving his room, but he didn't meet her eyes, instead preferring to shuffle papers around on his desk. Once in her own consulting room, she closed the door behind her, leaning against it a second, thinking about everything that had just taken place. Looking at her reflection in the mirror, she groaned and quickly tucked the wispy strands of strawberry blonde hair behind her ear. They always came loose, especially when Connor pulled at them with his chubby little hands. Thank goodness her lipstick wasn't all over her face but she wished she'd looked better, especially after meeting her new colleague. She looked like a harried mother instead of a professional general practitioner.

Not that it mattered now. Nathan had seen her all dishevelled and disorderly so there was nothing she could do about that, but for the first time since Bruce had left, she'd been acutely aware she was a woman. It was the way he'd held her hand that had caused a resurgence of the tinglings she hadn't experienced in an awful long time. And the way he'd smiled at her! There was no denying that Nathan Young had reminded her that she wasn't just a doctor, wasn't just a daughter, wasn't just a mother…she was a woman.

In a mad hurry, Morena pulled her long hair from its ponytail and ran her fingers through it, before quickly braiding it back away from her face. Rushing to her bag, she hunted around for her mascara and blush and ended up tipping the contents onto her desk in order to find them. Returning to the mirror, it took less than a minute to add the small dash of make-up that helped her feel more in control of what was happening.

She'd just returned to her desk when there was a knock at her door. Quickly, she began shoving everything back into her bag.

'Come in,' she called.

'Morena.' Nathan's voice stopped her and she looked up, embarrassed that she'd been caught primping. 'Do you have a spare box of 5-mil syringes?'

'Uh.' She dropped what she'd been holding and crossed to her cupboard. 'Sorry. I thought your consulting room was completely stocked. I'll get Sally to go through it once we've finished morning clinic.' She located the box of syringes and turned to hand it to him. He was staring at her desk, at the items still scattered all over it, among them a box of nursing pads. 'Here you are.'

'What? Sorry.' He looked up and took the syringes from her. 'Thanks.' A moment later he was gone. Morena sighed and shook her head. What must he think of her? First she was late, then she was flirty and now vain about her appearance.

'It doesn't matter what he thinks,' she told herself sternly as she finished clearing her desk of the clutter and picking up the large stack of patient files sitting on the corner of her desk, checking her list for the morning. 'Concentrate and get to work. Nathan Young is nothing more than a new colleague here to help you out.' With that, she pressed the button on her intercom and told Sally to send her first patient through.

The morning progressed, with Morena seeing her usual female patients as well as a few new ones. Having qualifications in women's health with a strong focus on ob/gyn and paediatrics, most of the pregnant women in Victor Harbor came to her for their prenatal care, some transferring to Adelaide when close to their due dates, others preferring to have their babies delivered at Victor Harbor hospital and yet others opting for natural birth at home, with just Morena there to deliver.

When her last patient had left, Morena headed to the little kitchen to get another cup of tea. She breathed in as she entered the room. 'Mmm. A freshly brewed pot of *chai*. My favourite. Sally,' she called. 'I love you.'

'I was the one who made the tea.' Nathan came striding into the room, filling it with his presence. His scent mingled with the spices from the *chai* and it was a heady aroma.

'Oh. Well. Thank you. I guess it's you I love, then.' The words were a throw-away line but as they tumbled out of her mouth she wondered if he'd take them the wrong way. Pouring herself some *chai* from the pot, she shook her head, deciding to forget it. If Nathan had a problem with her, he'd either have to tell her or deal with it himself. Her bad break-up with Bruce had shown her that she didn't need to justify every single one of her actions to every person she came into contact with.

'I guess it is.' Nathan put his cup on the bench and as the pot was still in her hand, she filled his mug. 'Thanks.'

'So how was your morning?'

He thought. 'Busy.' He thought some more. 'Interesting.' He studied her for a moment. 'Not as full of gossip as you'd earlier predicted.'

'Good for you, then.'

'How about you?'

'Ugh. Vaginal speculums coming out of my ears...which isn't the prettiest of pictures to present but at least women are having regular pap smears so I shouldn't be complaining.' She sat down at the table and sipped her tea. 'Mmm. Good *chai*, Nathan.'

'So...' He hesitated a moment as he pulled out a chair. 'Your patients are predominantly female?'

'Yes. It's stereotypical but it's the way society works. It's the main reason we needed to employ a male GP and also someone who was well qualified at the other end of the spectrum.'

'Sorry?'

'I see the young pregnant women, you see the menopausal ones.' She laughed at that. 'Not that they'd mind. The way you had Mrs Henderson eating out of your hand this morning, it's as though you have a real gift in that area.' As she babbled on, it took a while for her to realise that Nathan was looking at her as though she had two heads. 'Problem?'

'Pregnant women?'

'Oh, I was just generalising. You do get to see male patients as well and, of course, if an expectant mother prefers you to monitor her prenatal care, that's fine. I'm not precious about my patients. I just expect them to receive the best professional care this practice can provide.'

When he didn't comment, she decided to get things moving. 'Right, now, as I understand it, you've already registered at the hospital, been issued with your security pass, and so on?' He nodded and Morena continued, 'OK, then, I'm not sure whether my father gave you a clear indication of your schedule at the interview but you get this afternoon off and Dad will do the clinic.'

'I'm more than happy to work,' Nathan offered.

'It's not that.' Morena smiled. 'We're also big on not getting burnt out in this practice. Doctors are the worst at working themselves into the ground and from the day my father started this practice, he always insisted that each staff member had at least half a day off a week, not including weekends. At least this afternoon you can finish getting settled into your new apartment or just get to know the layout of the town.' She shrugged. 'Whatever takes your fancy.'

Nathan nodded, not looking forward to this enforced time off. He was the type of man who preferred to stay busy, to keep not only his body but his mind as active as possible. He was already settled into his apartment, which was just down the street from the clinic, and had no need of this free time Morena was talking about. However, it was hardly relevant to what she was saying. 'Anything else?'

'We also do quite a few house calls during the week. Some of these are to nursing homes, some to retirement villages and some to individual homes. For the next few weeks, my father and I thought it better if you and I did them together—that way you get to know more of our patients. Then, when you're more settled, we can split them up.'

'And what happens to the clinics one of us would usually be running?'

'Dad will cover them for these first few weeks, which I think is good because it will help him to cut back slowly on his workload, rather than going cold turkey to his two afternoons a week. We also do a regular shift at the hospital, rotating with the other GP practices here in Victor, but, then, I'm sure my father mentioned that at the interview. Sally has the new schedule typed out for everyone so if you don't have a copy, she—'

'I have it,' he interjected.

'Good.'

'I recall your father mentioning that most of his patients were getting on in years.'

'Yes. Victor Harbor supports a large retiree population. The district nurse is a huge help with daily dressings et cetera for those patients who are housebound but still able to live by themselves.'

'Hearing him speak so fondly of his patients and also the main demographic was the reason I chose this practice in the first place.'

'That's nice. I do remember reading your résumé and was impressed with your extensive experience in age preventative care and palliative medicine. In fact, with your qualifications I'm surprised you're choosing a small private practice. You could have quite a thriving city practice, not to mention a senior position on staff at any hospital in Australia.'

Nathan was always asked that question but it was one that usually came a few weeks into his contract at the numerous small town practices he'd worked at. 'I like the variety.' It was his stock answer and it was all she was going to get.

Morena noticed the same mask from this morning slip into place over his features, his vibrant brown eyes losing their sparkle to become rather dull. He obviously didn't want to discuss anything so she let it go.

'Now, about the hours. Usually my father would start the clinics at nine o'clock, sometimes eight-thirty when necessary. Are you happy to do those hours?'

'That's fine. I'm usually awake rather early so I can keep that up.'

'Fantastic.'

'What about you? You're not usually awake early?'

Morena smiled. 'If you're referring to me being late this morning…well, I guess I should tell you it's a common occurrence.' She shrugged. 'It's just the way things go. I don't consciously plan to be late but…' She let the sentence hang.

'You sleep in?'

'Sleep? I wish. Oh, how I *long* for a decent sleep-in.'

'Then why are you—?'

Morena's phone shrilled to life and she took it out of her pocket and checked the display. It was her mother calling. 'Hi, Mum,' she said after connecting the call. 'What's wrong?' She waited a moment then groaned. 'OK. Yep. Do that. See you soon.'

'Problem?' Nathan asked as she put her phone away.

'No. It just means I'll be running late for my afternoon clinic, but it can't be helped.'

It appeared that, whatever was going on, she wasn't about to let him in on the details even though it would delay her. 'I'm more than willing to hang around and help,' he offered, and she shook her head but still didn't give an explanation. Then again, perhaps it was none of his business and although he might be intrigued by Morena Camden and the entire set-up here at the thriving seaside practice, he knew when to butt out.

'The um…décor here is…not what I expected.' He glanced

around the kitchen at the orange laminate bench, brown vinyl cupboards and purple linoleum floor. 'Very…'

'Seventies,' Morena finished with a smile.

'I take it you didn't decorate it?'

'No.'

'Ever thought of renovating?'

'Perish the thought,' she joked. 'Besides, how many people do you know who have purple linoleum? I doubt you could buy it today and yet I guarantee you that some interior designer is out there at this very moment, searching high and low for purple linoleum.'

Nathan smiled and she was glad to see it back, although she did note that it didn't quite reach his eyes. 'You're probably right. That's a no to the redecorating, then?'

'I don't think I've given it all that much thought. It's been this way for as long as I can remember so I guess I don't see the clashing colours.'

'You have an emotional bond with it.' He nodded as though he understood then opened his mouth to say something else but stopped and closed it again.

'What?'

'Nothing.'

'No, go on. Say what you were going to say. You think this place would benefit from a complete overhaul.'

'I wouldn't go that far but a bit of paint, a change in waiting-room furniture, redo the reception area…'

'And you've given this no thought at all.' Her lips twitched and his smile brightened.

'Just an impartial observation. That's all.'

'A lot of the patients like the clinic the way it looks. It's always been that way for them and it's comfortable. They don't take to change easily, not the ones who have lived here for thirty years or more.'

Nathan nodded. 'Small town mentality. I've encountered it before in other places I've worked and in most of them the word "progress" can be considered an obscenity.'

Morena threw back her head and laughed. 'You are spot on, Nathan. Oh, it's good to have you here. I do think that although the practice projects a professional image, it does seem like a bit of a time warp when you step through the door.'

'Well, if you want help or suggestions, I'm more than willing.'

'Good to know. Thanks.' She drained her cup and had just finished washing it up when the tinkle of the bell over the front door sounded.

'More patients?' Nathan raised his eyebrows.

'Probably my mother.'

'Only us,' came the call.

'See? In the kitchen,' Morena replied. 'Have you met my mother?'

'Yes. When I came down for the interview.'

'Right. Good.' Morena came around the table as her mother came in to view, holding Connor in her arms. 'Now, little man. What seems to be the problem?'

Nathan watched as the baby, which he guessed to be about six months old, went willing to Morena, snuggling close and whimpering a little at his first opportunity. Nathan's eyes widened as he took in the light blond hair and blue eyes of the boy. He recalled the nursing pads he'd seen on Morena's desk, remembered her comment about sleeplessness and watched as she kissed the downy head with such love as only a mother could feel.

Nathan shot to his feet and eyed her cautiously. 'You have a son?'

She looked up and smiled. 'Yes. This is Connor.'

'You have a son,' he repeated, shaking his head. The smile

slid from her face as she saw the pain and anguish which she'd glimpsed only momentarily that morning flood into his eyes. In the next instant he was gone, the front door of the clinic closing solidly behind him.

CHAPTER TWO

'WHAT was that all about?' Joyce asked as she sat down in the chair Nathan had just vacated.

'I have no idea.' Morena shook her head for emphasis, staring at the doorway as though she expected him to reappear at any moment. He didn't. Sighing, Morena sat down, cradling Connor to her. 'What's up with you, little man? Hmm?' He started to cry a little but she could tell it was all put on. Morena unbuttoned her shirt and shifted Connor into position so she could feed him.

'He's tired but he's just not settling,' Joyce offered, standing once again to wash Nathan's cup and pour herself some tea. 'Nathan seems nice…a little eccentric perhaps but nice nevertheless.'

'Yes,' Morena said, still concerned about him. He was obviously upset that she had a son but she had no clue why. 'Not my problem,' she said out loud, and shook her head again.

'What's not your problem, dear?'

'Nathan. I've got to stop myself from getting involved in other people's lives.'

'You're *expected* to get involved in their lives. You're a GP, darling.'

'I'm not Nathan's doctor and, besides, he's here for six

months to take the weight off Dad's shoulders and that's all I can focus on right now. No room for anything else in my life. The practice, Connor and myself. That's what I need to focus my energies on.'

'But you also have a gift for helping people. It's one of the reasons why you're such a good doctor.'

Morena sighed and frowned, not at all sure she agreed with her mother.

'You think there's something…wrong with Nathan? Emotionally?' Joyce continued. 'I wonder why he insisted on only a six-month contract? He does know the job here is a permanent position?'

'I'm sure Dad covered that with him at the interview but from what I can tell, Nathan wanted just six months and nothing more, and after Dad's last angina attack it was better than nothing. I think he'll do well here. He certainly has a knack with the more mature ladies. He had Mrs Henderson smiling this morning.'

'Really?' Joyce was astounded. 'Well, well, well. Perhaps he is just what we need.' She sipped her tea then looked intently at her daughter. 'You know what you need to do, don't you,' she stated rhetorically.

'What?'

'Convince Nathan to stay. For good.'

'Mum. No. His life is his life. As far as I'm concerned, he's a doctor who's filling a need in the practice. Nothing more.'

'I'm not asking you to get involved with him on a personal level, Morena, although he's certainly very nice to look at. *Very* nice,' Joyce added with emphasis.

'Mum!'

Joyce chuckled. 'Oh, settle down. I'm only teasing. I know you don't want another man in your life, especially after the mess the last one made.'

Morena rolled her eyes at her mother's comment. They'd often discussed Bruce and how badly he'd treated her but she also didn't want to dwell on it. She was moving forward with her life, she wasn't looking back, and she certainly wasn't looking for another man. Complications she could do without, thank you very much. And even thinking of Nathan in a romantic context for just a second was enough to shake her world. Her mind flicked to the handshake they'd shared that morning, the way he'd seemed to have some sort of hold over her and the way his scent was totally mesmerising. She closed her eyes and sighed, surprised at how easily she could recall his handsome face.

'Morena?'

Her eyes snapped open at her mother's voice.

'Are you all right?'

'I'm fine, Mum.' And she was. She was doing fine and she shouldn't even *think* of daydreaming about her new colleague, despite how charming and good-looking he was. Business. Their relationship was professional and businesslike and nothing more.

And that's the way Morena kept it. She saw Nathan around the clinic for the next few days between patients and once or twice bumped into him in the kitchen. Neither of them said anything about what had happened on Monday when he'd stalked out after finding out she had a son—and neither of them wanted to. Somehow they'd managed to find a polite but friendly balance of professionalism and she hoped it would stay like that…although for some strange reason she'd often found her thoughts turning to Nathan during the nights when she had been pacing the floor with her son. She wanted to know what had made him so sad, so aloof, and hoped there was some non-intrusive way she could help.

* * *

Thursday was the first of the house calls she would be doing with Nathan. After morning clinic and with her father settled in to do his stint, Morena started sorting out the files of the patients she'd be seeing. Nathan had gone out for a walk after finishing his patient list and Sally was having a difficult time trying to contact him.

'I can't reach him,' Sally said. 'Either he's switched his mobile off or he's out of range.'

Morena shook her head. 'He has to be out of range. There are so many places around here where reception is bad.'

'How do you know he didn't just switch it off?' Sally asked. 'You don't know anything about him, Morena.'

'He's a doctor,' she stated matter-of-factly. 'We'll be leaving in five minutes. I'll go finish packing my bag.'

'But he's not here,' Sally yelled after her retreating figure.

'He will be,' Morena called back with more assurance than she felt. She hoped she hadn't misjudged Nathan and silently willed him to come back to the clinic and prove her right.

Sighing, Morena forced herself to stop worrying about her colleague and concentrate on going over the files for the patients they would see that afternoon, packing the necessary medications.

'How long will house calls take?' Nathan's voice from her doorway made her start and she almost twisted her neck to look at him.

'About three hours today.'

'Usually less?'

'Yes.'

'More today because I'm the new kid on the block?'

'All shiny and ready to show off,' she agreed, snapping the bag closed. Nathan's mobile phone shrilled to life and he snapped it off his waistband.

'Dr Young.' He paused. 'Sally?' He looked over his

shoulder in the direction of the waiting room. 'Where am I?' A puzzled smile spread across his lips. 'Just a moment. I'll check.' Without covering the handset, he said clearly and loudly, 'Morena? Where am I?'

'Standing in my doorway.' She, too, was grinning. Poor Sally. Nathan had obviously come in the back door and she'd completely forgotten to tell the receptionist he was here.

Nathan took the phone from his ear and looked at it. 'She hung up.'

'Why didn't someone tell me he'd been found?' Sally came storming down the corridor and both doctors burst out laughing before apologising.

'We'd better get going.' Morena picked up her bag and keys and headed out to the front where she'd left her car. 'Thanks, Sally.'

As they headed out to the car, Morena glanced at Nathan and said quickly, 'I just need to stop off and see my mother, then we'll be on our way.'

'Why do you need to see your mother?'

'Well…it's Connor, really. I just want to check on him.' She put her bag in the back of the car before sliding into the driver's seat. 'He hasn't been himself lately. Just niggling, nothing *really* wrong. It's probably just teething.'

Nathan couldn't believe how uncomfortable he felt and wondered if he could stay in the car. Since he'd first discovered she was a single mother, he'd avoided the subject and the thoughts they brought like the plague. He wasn't good around babies. 'I'm sure Joyce will be fine with him. After all, she has had a bit of experience when it comes to motherhood.'

'Connor is my son and I don't care if people call me neurotic or paranoid or whatever—if I want to go check on him, I'm going to go check on him.'

Nathan shrugged and buckled up his seat belt as she started

the engine. 'The job description mentioned rotational duties at the hospital. How does that work when you have a young baby?'

'My parents have Connor when the practice is rostered on.'

'You don't feel he needs more of your time?'

'I'm a single mother, Nathan. I need to work. Chances are things may change later when Connor's older, but for now he spends time with his grandparents.'

'Another reason for your father to slow down.' He nodded at this, coming to the conclusion himself.

'Are you concerned about my performance as a general practitioner or as a mother?'

'Neither. I'm just trying to gauge how much time I may need to spend around pregnant women or young babies.' He crossed his arms and Morena noted his defensive posture as she reversed out of the clinic car park.

'Don't like treating them?'

'Everyone has their sub-speciality. You've already stated mine.'

'And mine is pregnant women and young families. That's why we blend well here at the clinic. At the hospital, it's the general range of A and E complaints. Several of the local GPs share the on-call duties at the hospital. Our practice is on every fourth weekend. You did say you'd collected your hospital security pass?'

'Yes. I have to say I was surprised a small hospital such as Victor Harbor had such strict security measures.'

Morena breathed a small sigh of relief, glad they were back onto a more general topic. It wasn't her place to get involved in his life, his problems. If he wanted to talk, she would be there to listen, but she was through getting so deeply involved in people's lives that she ended up losing herself. It had been what had happened with Bruce and her emotional loss of identity was something she was determined never to put herself through again.

'The hospital has the usual security passes and codes but it's been intensified in the last six months due to the excessive number of…shall we call them *visitors* from Adelaide and elsewhere around the state, who come to Victor Harbor on the weekend and imbibe far too much alcohol.'

'There have been bad incidents?'

'Yes. Also, after school breaks up for the summer holidays, the students who have completed high school all come here for a huge party. Personally, I'm glad that's over for another year.'

'You didn't enjoy it?'

'Put it this way, the gastric lavage unit didn't enjoy it.'

'Ah.'

Morena tipped her head to the side and indicated his mouth. 'Is that a smile?'

'No.'

'Right.' She didn't sound as though she believed him. Her parents didn't live far from the clinic so it was but a few minutes before she was pulling into their driveway. As she climbed from the car, she noted that Nathan hadn't moved. 'You don't want to come in? Say hello to Mum?'

'I don't want to hold us up,' he said, and she took the hint.

'OK, then. I'll be quick.' As she walked up the front path of the house she'd grown up in, she frowned, trying to figure him out. He was a puzzle, that was for certain, but she also knew it was one she shouldn't touch. She'd found Bruce intriguing, exciting and she'd been overawed. No. It wasn't happening again. She didn't care how shiny yet broken Nathan Young appeared, she was *not* going to get involved with him. There was no way her heart could take another beating.

As she walked in the front door, calling out to her mother, Morena heard her son start to niggle. Joyce came towards her.

'Hi, darling.'

'Won't stop long. Nathan's out in the car.'

'He didn't want to come in?'

'I don't think he wants me to be too long so we don't get behind on the house calls.'

'Ah...a wise man.'

Morena headed over to where her son was lying on the floor, rolling over and over, one hand in his mouth. Picking him up, she kissed his forehead. 'Temperature's gone at least.'

'He's still not settling properly,' Joyce pointed out. 'It could be his ears.'

'True. Has he been tugging on them?'

'No. Just shoving his fist in his mouth or chewing on his teething rattle.'

'I'll take my otoscope home tonight and check his ears then,' Morena decided, cuddling Connor close. The baby snuggled into his mother and closed his eyes.

'So how are things going with Nathan?' Joyce's eyes were bright with teasing excitement.

'Good.'

'That's not all there is to it. I know you, Morena. I know that look on your face, that look in your eyes. You're intrigued by this one. You can see he's broken and you want to fix him, just as you fixed all your toys when you were little.'

'Nathan's hardly a toy, Mum.' She didn't bother to deny it. No one could read her as clearly as her mother could.

'So what do you think is wrong?'

She shrugged nonchalantly. 'He doesn't like babies.'

'Really?' Joyce reached out and rubbed Connor's downy head. 'How is that possible?'

'It has been known to happen, Mother.' Morena smiled and

kissed her son's head. It was then she realised he'd fallen asleep. 'I'll go put him down,' she said, and headed into the bedroom, returning quickly. 'I'd better get going.'

Joyce came out with her and said hello to Nathan, telling him not to be a stranger and to drop in any time.

'Thanks. That's very kind.'

'Oh, we want to make you so happy here that you never want to leave Victor Harbor, don't we, Morena?' she ventured.

'Quite so, Mother,' Morena said as if on cue.

'I know,' Joyce said brightly. 'Why don't you come around on the weekend, if you're free? It's not our turn to work at the hospital so if you don't have anything else planned, we'll have a good old-fashioned country barbeque. The weather is supposed to be perfect for it.'

'Thank you for the invitation,' he said as Morena started the engine. 'I'll let you know.'

Neither of them spoke as they waved goodbye to her mother and started heading to their first destination. 'Where to?' Nathan asked, picking up the patient files.

'First stop is Holland Nursing Home, named for the late James Holland, who was a real pioneer in these parts.'

'A history lesson to go with the house calls. Nice.'

'We aim to please!' She parked the car in the special spot reserved for doctors. 'The easiest way to see all the patients is to do a ward round and then go back to any specific patients if necessary.'

'You bring all their patient files with you?'

'No. The files I have are for the other calls we need to make.'

'Ever thought of updating the practice into the computer age?'

Morena nodded. 'Quite frequently. Now's just not the right time.'

'Hands tied by your dad?'

'Something like that.'

Morena entered the nursing home and introduced Nathan to the staff. The three female nursing sisters on duty instantly brightened at his presence and she was astounded to see the effect he had on members of the opposite sex. Was that what she had looked like on Monday morning when he'd rescued her from Mrs Henderson's attack? All gooey and turning to mush at the simplest smile from him? He did have a smile that brightened up the entire place so why shouldn't he use it? Sneaking a sidelong glance at him, Morena realised he knew full well the power of his smile and she wouldn't put it past him to use it when it suited him.

Charm. Charisma. Grace. Manners. The man had them all—in spades. She could recognise the traits because Bruce had had the same ones and she'd fallen for them—hook, line and sinker. She'd thought she'd been happy. She'd thought Bruce would change his mind about wanting a family…but he hadn't, and from the instant she'd told him she was pregnant, he'd changed. The man with the charm, the man who had made her believe he would give her the world, the man she'd fallen in love with, had changed and become a stranger overnight.

'How many beds?' Nathan asked.

'What?' Morena was startled out of her reverie and looked at her new colleague blankly.

'Are you all right?'

'Yeah. Sorry. What did you say?'

'You were miles away.' He seemed intrigued and concerned at the same time and she wondered why. He was nothing to her just as she was nothing to him. Colleagues. That's all. He was there to help out at the practice so her father could get his much-needed rest. They could become professional friends, that was all right, but nothing beyond that. So why did he seem to care so much? Was it polite? Was it real? Was it just part of his charming act?

'I was.' From somewhere she managed to dredge up the question he'd asked. 'Um…thirty-seven.'

'Why do they always have to go with the odd numbers?' he asked rhetorically. 'Why not go for a full forty?'

'It started out as a thirty-bed home but it's grown. No doubt we'll hit forty soon enough, although where we'd fit three extra beds, I'm still trying to figure out.' She walked towards the first room and they began the ward round.

As they continued to meet one patient after the next, some having suffered strokes, two with Parkinson's and several with dementia, Morena watched as Nathan charmed one after the other. He was very good with each of them, making them feel as though he was there for only them and no one else.

His face was filled with animated delight as they continued to do the rounds. 'He's brilliant,' one of the nurses said softly as he spoke with Mrs Matthews. 'So caring and natural.'

'Yes,' Morena agreed, highly impressed.

'Ooh, he's a nice one, Dr Camden,' Mrs Matthews said, slurring her words slightly. She was still having extensive rehabilitation for the stroke she'd suffered, but her mind was as sharp as ever. 'Thank you for bringing him along.'

'My pleasure.' Morena smiled, watching as Nathan checked their patient's eyes.

'It's been a long time since I've had a young, handsome man looking into my eyes.'

They all chuckled as Nathan straightened. 'And it's been a long time since I've met a woman who's not afraid to be forward.'

Morena said softly, 'My guess is, you'll be meeting a few more of them.'

Nathan ignored her and gave Mrs Matthews one of his

Prince Charming smiles, and if she hadn't been lying in bed, she probably would have fallen down due to the way her knees would have weakened. As it was, Morena rested her hand on the chair beside the bed just to make sure *she* didn't fall down.

By the time they'd finished at the Holland Nursing Home, they were half an hour behind. 'Your fault,' Morena said as she pulled out onto the road that led to the Bluff.

'Why is that?'

'Well, you *would* flirt with every female in the place.' As soon as she'd said the words, she realised that Nathan might actually take it the wrong way, think she was cross with him or even chastising him, but his response let her know they were definitely on the same wavelength.

'Are you jealous? After all, you did tell me on Monday that you loved me.'

'So I did.' She nodded slowly, then looked over at him and laughed. His eyebrows were raised, his eyes were bright and twinkling and his lips were curved into a slight but interested smile.

'Oh, I'm definitely jealous but it's healthy to have competition where affairs of the heart are concerned, and I'm sure Mrs Matthews and the others will give me a run for my money.'

'I believe she will.' Nathan was silent for a moment before asking quietly, 'Is that what happened with you?'

'What? Mrs Matthews giving me a run for my money?'

'No. I meant did your husband have an affair?'

'Oh.' The laughter disappeared from her face. 'Yes.' She put her indicator on and turned the corner. Why had he done that? Why had he gone and spoilt a nice camaraderie with a personal question? She was equally as curious about him and interested to know how the pain she'd seen in his eyes had been caused.

'I'm not usually this inquisitive, or intrusive,' Nathan

added, 'but there's something about you that just doesn't seem to add up.'

'And that's a problem?'

'Not professionally.'

'I'm odd?' Again she looked over at him.

'You have a child.'

'And how is that odd? Many women have children.'

'You have more than one?'

'No. No. Just Connor. I meant that it's not an uncommon occurrence for a thirty-year-old woman to also be a mother.' She paused. 'What about you? Any children hiding in your closet?'

Nathan turned away and looked out the window, not appreciating the dry South Australian landscape before him. He should have expected it, he realised. He'd asked her a personal question so he should have expected one in return. The green foliage of the gum trees flashed by in a haze as they continued on their journey. 'No,' he finally answered.

'See? You're doing it again. You're asking questions and wanting to know about my life but you're not willing to tell me anything about yours.' She slowed the car and pulled into a tree-lined dirt road where the houses were few and far between and the farms of the district began. Neither of them spoke until she'd pulled up outside an old stone cottage where the grass was only green in patches due to the drought still plaguing the land. Undoing her seat belt, she turned to face him.

'Bruce left me because I was pregnant. He didn't want children. He told me that before we got married but I assumed he'd change his mind. He didn't. The fact that he had affairs also didn't help, but it's all in the past. The only problem is the people of this town, with all their gossip, make it very difficult for me to move forward.'

'Perhaps they never liked him in the first place.' Nathan finally turned to look at her.

'Perhaps. Anyway, that's the story. Nothing big or fancy. I just married the wrong person. That's all.'

'And now you're on your own. A single mother.'

'That's right.'

'He left when the baby was born?'

'No. He left when I refused to have an abortion.' With the taste of her failed marriage rising up in her throat, she grabbed her medical bag from the back and climbed from the car, stalking angrily towards the house.

When he entered the house, Nathan found Morena smiling at her patients, although he noted that the smile didn't meet her eyes the way it had earlier and he knew he was to blame for its loss. He wasn't quite sure why he'd pushed so hard to make her say the words. Perhaps he felt that once they were out in the open, their strange friendship might settle down. He really wasn't sure what to make of Morena Camden—a woman who was running a busy medical practice while also raising a child. That took guts and he appreciated that. Still, why had he felt compelled to push?

Because he wanted to know more about her.

The answer came to him in a flash, as though his head and his heart were warring with each other, the heart wanting to acknowledge the sensations he felt when he looked at Morena, when he watched her walk, when he heard her laughter. His head, on the other hand, was more than happy to ignore everything and continue playing the game of guilt it had started long ago.

'Nathan.' Morena beckoned him over. 'Come and meet two amazing people.'

Nathan walked towards the elderly couple who Morena introduced as Beatrice and Benedick. Beatrice was petite, with white hair flowing down to her shoulders and tied up with a bright red ribbon. Benedick was sitting in a chair, an oxygen cylinder beside him on the right and two cups of tea on the table to his left. The house was cosy but it was the people in front of him who captured Nathan's attention.

'You do realise your names are from—?' Nathan said, his eyes alight, and Beatrice cut him off.

'We've been together for almost sixty years, young man. Don't you think it's occurred to us before now that our names are from *Much Ado About Nothing*?'

'Why do you think I chose her?' Benedick chimed in, coughing as he spoke. 'Couldn't go past my Beatrice and we didn't have any problems getting together, like our namesakes.' He gazed fondly into the woman's eyes and Nathan couldn't believe what he was witnessing. Such love, such devotion and for such a long time.

'All right. Break it up, you two lovebirds.' Morena put her bag on the floor and snapped it open.

Benedick chuckled and coughed again. 'Here, drink your tea,' Beatrice said, handing him a cup, her hand shaking from the Parkinson's which obviously was starting to wage war on her body.

'How has he been, Beatrice? You haven't called me so I'm presuming everything's been all right? Medication's working?'

'You can talk to me directly,' Benedick said darkly as he drained his teacup.

'I'll ask you all about her, OK?'

'Quizzing me to see if I can remember things or to see how well I know my wife?' he wanted to know.

'Why not both?' Morena asked.

'Ah, it's the first one. Checking my memory. She's a sneaky one, this girly is. Always was,' Benedick said to Nathan, coughing once more. 'Known her since before she was born, I have, and from the instant her mother showed her to me, I said, "This one's gonna be sneaky." And I was right.'

Morena withdrew a stethoscope from her bag and handed it to Nathan. 'Make yourself useful.'

'Right you are, boss.'

Benedick started to complain but Beatrice shushed him. 'How can the doctor listen to your lungs if you're blathering on? I don't know. As bad as ever. Now, sit down, deary.' She took Morena's hand and guided her to a chair. 'The medication you have him on has been working a treat. The coughing's not as intense and he can cope much better. I've made him use the oxygen more frequently, like you suggested, and although he complains he can see the benefit of it.'

'I don't comp—'

'Shush,' both women said in unison, then smiled at each other.

'I've kept an eye on him—'

'More than an eye,' Benedick interrupted again, waggling his eyebrows up and down.

'Shush!' All three said, and the old man merely started laughing, which ended up in a coughing fit. Morena fitted the oxygen non-rebreather mask over his mouth and nose while Nathan turned the tank on and within a few seconds Benedick was calm again.

'You do like being the centre of attention, don't you?' Morena lifted his wrist and took his pulse. 'Better. I think we'll keep you on the same medication for the next few days. Nathan will be doing your house calls from now on so if you have any problems, he's the one you call in the middle of the night.'

'Little Connor been keeping you up?' Beatrice asked. 'I heard from your mother that he's been giving you a bit of trouble.'

'He's had a bit of a cold and colic.'

'Aw, nothing that a mother's love can't fix.' Beatrice nodded knowingly and pointed to the main photograph on the wall. It was a picture taken at a studio of the two of them surrounded by children, grandchildren and great-grandchildren. 'Trust me, I know.'

'I *do* trust you but after four nights of no sleep I begin to wonder if he's ever going to grow out of this stage.'

'He will. Don't you worry. You're doing a good job. We're all right proud of you.'

'Thank you.' Morena was all choked with emotion at Beatrice's words and she bent down, pretending to rummage in her bag while she pulled herself together. Nathan kept glancing over at her as he finished with Benedick's check-up, seeing how difficult things were for her. Within half a minute she straightened, her features composed as she began Beatrice's check-up.

After they'd finished the medical part of their visit, they stayed for a quick cup of tea where, although they were chatting about general topics, Nathan realised just how much information Morena managed to gather about what had really been happening between their two patients. Beatrice told of a fall she'd had because of a rug slipping and how one of her sons had come and stuck the rug to the floor with double-sided tape.

'He wanted to go out and buy me a new non-slip rug thing but I really like that one.'

'It took us so long to choose, you'd better still like it,' Benedick added, his breathing now quite settled.

'Anyway, I'm glad he was able to fix it. I'm sorry I don't have any biscuits to offer you. I was supposed to do cooking with my granddaughter yesterday but she wasn't feeling too well. Did she come and see you this morning?'

'She did,' Morena acknowledged. 'She should be as right as rain by next week. Nothing to worry about.'

'She said if she came, she might pass on her germs to Benedick and that wouldn't do him any good.'

'No. She was very wise. You're still having trouble in the kitchen, then? How many times do Meals-on-Wheels deliver?'

'Three times a week but don't worry about us. I can make tea and the kids take turns at making us meals and bringing them over to freeze.'

'They bought us a new big freezer for Christmas,' Benedick told Nathan, and shook his head. 'I raised them to be practical but I didn't think they'd turn out *that* practical.'

'Shush. You're only upset that you didn't get as many toys this year as you did last year,' his wife responded. 'The freezer is just right and it does help a great deal with the meals. They're good kids we have.'

'You know you're getting old when your kids give you antacids and medication for your birthday and a freezer as a Christmas present.' Benedick chuckled and thankfully didn't cough. Nathan laughed along, amazed at these two wonderful people Morena had introduced him to.

'They're living proof,' he said after they finally said goodbye and headed on to the next house call, both of them glad of the air-conditioning in the car, a cool respite from the searing summer heat.

'Proof of what?'

'That true love exists.'

Morena was surprised. 'You sound as though you don't believe in true love. You're a cynic?'

Nathan opened his mouth to say something then closed it again. After a moment of deep contemplation he said slowly, 'I wouldn't call myself a cynic but it's not often I've seen people get their happily ever after.'

'My parents did and I do see a lot of people around here who are like Beatrice and Benedick but none of them are as gorgeous, I have to admit.'

'Almost sixty years, though. That's a long time to spend with one person.'

'It's just like a fairy-tale.' Morena sighed. 'It gives me hope.'

'Hope?'

'Hope that things will turn out right for me.'

'You want to get married again?' His tone was incredulous.

'I want my life to be happy,' she countered.

'You haven't been put off by what happened?'

Morena stopped the car at their next house call. Staring straight ahead, she answered thoughtfully, 'I'm cautious. I'm careful. I'm more wise when it comes to what I want and who I want to share that with, but I'm also sure I don't want to be alone for the rest of my life.'

'You at least have your son.' The words were spoken softly with pain and bitterness threaded through them. 'At least you were left with him.'

This time it was Nathan who exited the car first, leaving Morena to wonder at the anguish in his voice.

Was it possible that somehow Nathan had lost a child?

CHAPTER THREE

IT ALL made perfect sense. Nathan's reaction when he'd seen Connor, his reaction to the number of pregnant women and small children the practice looked after. His words continued to plague her throughout the night. 'At least you have your son.' Morena shifted closer in the queen-sized bed to where her son lay. Tonight she'd found it easier just to put him on the mattress beside her, rather than walking around with him until he went to sleep. Tonight she needed comfort and Nathan was right—she *did* have Connor and she never wanted to forget that or take her son for granted.

'You were worth the pain. Worth the anguish,' she whispered to her sleeping child as she stroked his soft head. 'How could Bruce ever suggest getting rid of you? The man was insane.' And that was the truth of the matter. It had caused a lot of ripples in her life since he'd walked out, and not only of a personal nature.

When she and Bruce had returned to Victor Harbor to help out in the family practice, they'd invested a lot of money into it. When Bruce had left, he'd insisted on being paid out in full. It was something she'd managed to keep to herself, to not let her parents know about it, but it had meant taking out another loan, one which she was still trying to figure out the best way to pay back.

She'd sold the house they'd bought together, giving Bruce half of the proceeds, and had purchased the small apartment three houses down from her parents, telling them she wanted to be closer and that it was best for Connor—which was absolutely true.

'You come first,' she told him. 'You're the most important man in my life and I love you so much, my darling. It'll all work out right in the end. Just you wait and see. You'll be proud of your mummy.' Morena brushed the silent tears from her eyes and gathered Connor into her arms, breathing in his scent and relaxing. 'Everything will be all right,' she sighed, and closed her eyes.

'She's late again.' Nathan picked up the files he needed off Sally's desk. 'Is she always late?'

'It depends on how badly Connor slept. When babies have colic or start teething or both, it's rare that the mums get a good night's sleep. Sometimes, if her clinic is light, I send her home for an hour to two to rest while I watch Connor.'

'That's very decent of you.'

'We're a family practice.' Sally smiled at him.

'I didn't know that pertained to the staff.'

'We look after each other, all right. In fact, when my husband was involved in a car accident a few years back, Morena and her mother were my lifeline. They kept a close eye on everything that was happening at the hospital, brought me meals, made sure I looked after myself, and Morena even went and cleaned my house so that when Sean was finally released from hospital, it was one less thing I had to worry about. Oh, we're a family all right and in being such a close unit we can provide the same sort of community atmosphere to our patients.'

'Sorry!' Morena burst through into the waiting room,

coming in from the back door, her bag falling off her shoulder as she came round the receptionist's desk. 'Hi, Nathan,' she said breathlessly, hoping her hair didn't look as bad as she thought it did.

'Another bad night?' Sally asked.

'No. We both slept in. He was up around two o'clock but after I got him settled I forgot to check the alarm.' She grinned sheepishly at her colleagues. 'Nothing like waking up with a start and realising you're late to get the blood pumping.'

'Nothing like it,' Nathan murmured, as the bell over the door tinkled and their first patients for the day entered. Morena was a total whirlwind and from what he'd observed over the past week, it appeared she was like this in most parts of her life. She was either moving or she was still. There was no slow motion in between. Her hair, which she'd obviously pulled back into a loose ponytail, had tendrils hanging down by her face, making her appear far younger than he knew her to be. Although there were faint dark circles under her eyes, the bright blue of her irises sparkled with a love of life. In short, she made quite a picture, even in her haphazardness.

'Whew, it's hot out there,' Mrs Malcolm said, fanning herself with a piece of paper. 'Heard on the radio it's gonna be a right royal scorcher t'day.'

'Would you like a glass of water?' Morena offered as she hoisted her bag onto her shoulder and picked up her files.

'That'd be great, darlin'. Thanks so much.'

'I'll get it for you,' Sally said as Kira Davies, who was almost to term, waddled into the room, also fanning herself.

'Go on through, Kira. I won't be long,' Morena instructed so the woman didn't have to sit down and then get up again. She knew how difficult and uncomfortable it could be to do the simplest of things in those last few weeks of pregnancy, especially in this type of heat.

'I'll go stand under the air-conditioning vent,' Kira said as she headed through to Morena's consulting room.

Morena was hemmed in behind the receptionist desk, Sally having gone to get Mrs Malcolm a glass of water. She had her Tuesday patient files in her arms, her bag on her shoulder and Nathan blocking her way. 'How have you been?' she asked after a moment, when it appeared he was in no hurry to move.

'Good. Fine. You?'

'Same.'

'Connor?'

'He seems to be picking up a little, so I'm thinking it's just been his teeth that was making him under the weather.'

'And the colic?'

'Settled.'

'Good.'

No one spoke. It was as though there was this huge void between them—the void from their pasts. There was no denying that every time they'd been in the same room as each other, moments like this happened. The two of them standing there, looking at each other, breathing each other in and taking stock of the little quirky things the other did. For example, Morena had observed that Nathan stirred his tea clockwise and his coffee anti-clockwise. Silly little things like that, but it was the silly little things she was coming to like about him.

Neither was willing to make the first move, to break the connection, the unspoken conversation they appeared to be having, and while it was quite a strange sort of relationship, it was one they both seemed happy with…for now. Usually when she was this close to him she tended to babble a little due to the way he unnerved her. Today seemed to be the exception. They continued just to look at each other. His close proximity, the way he was looking at her as though she were a big shiny package, the scent of aftershave mixed with the flowers on the desk and the air-conditioning all started to make her a little light-headed, which was the last thing she needed.

Sally returned with Mrs Malcolm's water and turned to face the two doctors.

'What are you still doing there? Get to work.'

It was then Nathan looked away from Morena, a little startled he'd been just standing there, staring at his colleague—with a patient watching them intently. He shifted and gathered up his own files. 'Mrs Malcolm. Come on through,' he said, and stalked towards his consulting room, wondering if he'd be able to concentrate at all.

He had no idea what Morena was doing to him. No idea how a woman he hardly knew could invade his dreams the way she'd been doing since they'd met last week. They were good dreams…dreams he was happy enough to continue with…but the fact still remained that it was wrong. He wasn't available… not emotionally speaking. Although he'd been a widower for over ten years now, he still carried the haunting memory of his wife with him wherever he went, or at least he had until he'd arrived in Victor Harbor and met Morena Camden.

The rest of the day continued without Morena seeing much more of Nathan, even though she hung around the kitchen at lunchtime, hoping for another glimpse of him. More than once she'd heard the sounds of laughter coming from his consulting room and was pleased he was getting on well with the patients. He seemed easygoing and friendly and that was fantastic as far as the practice went, but personally she now knew he was hiding a deep sadness and although she didn't know the particulars, it was still enough to concern her.

'You're too emotive,' she mumbled to herself as she packed her bag for the afternoon house calls. Today it was mainly quick antenatal checks for a few of the mums who found it difficult for a number of reasons to make it to the clinic. Either they had no means of transport or they had other children to care for. It was also the day she could take Connor with her and she enjoyed being able to spend that extra time with him.

The door to Nathan's consulting room swung open and as hers was just as wide, she looked up in time see him chatting animatedly with Mr Ood.

'And then she stepped on the ball!' Mr Ood delivered the punchline and both men laughed. Morena breathed in, allowing the rich, deep sounds of Nathan's laughter to wash over her, and amazingly found she liked the feeling very much. She watched as the two men walked out to the reception area, neither looking her way.

Quickly, she checked her reflection in the mirror, waiting for Nathan to return, but he didn't. Puzzled, she headed out to the waiting room only to find it empty, with Sally sitting at the desk.

'You still here?'

'Yes. Just about to go.' She frowned. 'I thought I heard Nathan out here.'

'Oh, yeah. You did. He's just gone home to get some lunch.'

Morena's eyebrows hit her hairline. 'Home? How far away does he live?'

'Just down the street.'

'No wonder he's here at the crack of dawn,' she muttered. 'I didn't know that.'

'Oh. Well, he lives about three doors down so he can just walk to and from work any time he wants. I thought you knew. Edward found him the apartment.'

'He did? I didn't know that either.'

'I guess things have been pretty hectic in your life of late so it's no surprise that other things have escaped your notice. Anyway, your mother called to say that Connor's awake but I thought you'd gone so I told her you were on your way.'

'Right. Right.' Morena shook her head to clear it. Nathan had managed to fill a lot of her free thoughts that morning and it shouldn't be the case. 'I'm going now.' Gathering her things together, she headed out the back door to her car.

'Why should it feel so lonely in the car?' she asked her son as they drove from one house to the next. 'I already miss his big, bulky presence in the car.' Morena shook her head. 'I'm going insane, Connor. Your mumma is quietly going cuckoo.' She glanced at her son, sitting in his child safety seat in the rear of the car, and smiled as he gurgled back as if to say he knew but he still loved her.

As she pulled into the driveway of her last house call, her mobile phone rang and she quickly answered it. 'Dr Camden.'

'Morena.' Nathan's deep voice filled her senses and she closed her eyes as it washed over her. How could this man have such an effect on her? Then again, she'd always been partial to deep voices. There was silence. 'Are you there? Hello?'

Now she was forgetting to speak. 'I'm here. Sorry. Is there a problem?'

'I've finished for the day and wondered if you required any help with the house calls.'

'You've finished already?'

'Last patient cancelled.'

'Who was that?'

'Mr Dinsmore.'

Morena shook her head. 'He's just making an excuse. I'm on my last house call so if you can meet me in about ten minutes at Mr Dinsmore's, we'll see him together.'

'Sally said he made another appointment.'

'Not good enough. He needs to be seen today. He's been putting it off for far too long.'

Nathan was surprised at her vehemence but decided to

question it later. 'I'll read up on his notes and meet you. What's the address?' He wrote it down and said goodbye. A few minutes later he could see why Morena was so insistent that Ron Dinsmore be seen. He suffered from high blood pressure and on quite a few occasions had forgotten to take his medication. Morena's father had enlisted the help of the district nurse to help with daily checks but it was noted that a lot of the time Mr Dinsmore refused to let her in, telling her he could look after himself without any help. The file also stated that he was beginning to suffer from memory loss.

'Sally, can you tell me where O'Callaghan Street is?'

'Two blocks from here.' She pointed in the direction. 'Mr Dinsmore?'

'Yes. Morena wants me to meet her there. As it's not too far, I'll walk.' Nathan returned to his consulting room and quickly packed up his things, then locked the door and said goodbye to Sally. As he counted the house numbers in O'Callaghan Street, he heard a car turn into the street and looked around to see Morena pulling up. He walked over, trying to ignore the spark of pleasure he felt at seeing her. They'd been like ships passing in the night with the hectic morning clinic, but he'd reminded himself that he wasn't there to ogle his new boss, he was there to help her out and earn his keep.

'Hi.' She climbed from the car, her medical bag in her hand. She walked around and placed it on the footpath, before returning to the car and opening the back door. Nathan watched, confused about what she was doing. A moment later he heard a little snuffling cry of protest and Morena cooing. She had her son with her! He felt the blood drain from his face. He'd accepted the fact that she had a child but he was also determined to keep his distance from the baby as just seeing him was enough to bring back a fresh round of haunting memories.

'You take your son on house calls?' The words were out of his mouth before he could stop them and as she turned with Connor on her hip, his eyes were drawn to the way her son snuggled into her shoulder, half-asleep. A deep yearning, large and painful, squeezed at his heart at the sight they made. Morena flicked her ponytail over her shoulder and bent to pick up the medical bag. It was enough to break Nathan from his trance and he quickly scooped up the bag for her.

'I only take him on Tuesdays, which is my antenatal check-up day. He likes it and we get to spend a bit more time together.' She dropped a kiss on his head. 'Even if he does tend to snooze most of the time.'

Nathan nodded, unable to speak for a moment. Thankfully Morena didn't seem to notice as she led the way through the neglected garden to the front door. She pressed the buzzer and waited. A few seconds later they heard shuffling towards the door. 'I hope he's in a good mood and lets us in.'

'People trying to hide don't usually like it when they're found.'

Morena heard the truth in his words and sneaked a glance at him, seeing his jovial mask slip a tiny bit before he put it back in place. Was that what he was doing in Victor Harbor? Was he hiding? Hiding from the pain of his past?

The front door opened a crack and Morena pasted on her best smile. 'Hi, Mr Dinsmore. Do you mind if we come in?'

'Yes, I do,' the man grumped.

'Oh. Well, it's not for me, it's for Connor here. It's time for him to have some food but I just need to warm it up first.'

'Then go home.'

Morena just laughed and shifted Connor, who now had his eyes wide open but was still snuggled beneath his mother's neck. 'We're here now so if you don't mind...' She edged forward, watching closely as Mr Dinsmore fixed his eyes on Connor, seeing him soften.

'All right but just for a few minutes until he's fed. Who's this?' He stabbed a gnarled finger in Nathan's direction.

'This is Dr Young. The doctor who's taking over from my father.' Morena was now inside the house and Nathan followed, keeping the medical bag down by his side and out of sight. 'You were supposed to have an appointment with him today but Sally mentioned you'd cancelled.'

'Wasn't feeling up to it.' The man shuffled through into the kitchen and sat at the table. 'There's the stove. Heat the food.'

Morena snapped her fingers. 'Oops. I've left his bag in the car. Here…' She held Connor out to the old man, not giving him the opportunity to refuse. If he didn't take the child, Connor would drop to the floor, but Morena had total confidence in the other man. He'd raised seven of his own children and now had a plethora of grandchildren. Unfortunately, none of them lived close and since his wife's death Mr Dinsmore had been all alone.

She breezed past Nathan, giving him a quick wink and whispered, 'Work your magic, Doctor.' She'd noticed enough of Nathan in the past week to know he had a gift when it came to connecting with his patients, and she knew when she returned to the house, after dawdling at the car on purpose, she would find Mr Dinsmore ready to do whatever was needed to ensure his health was maintained.

Five minutes later she came back in and was about to speak when she heard muted voices coming from the kitchen. Quietly she made her way to the homely room at the rear of the house, recalling the numerous times she'd been here as a child and the way Mrs Dinsmore had always had something scrumptious baking in the oven. Now, the place seemed… forlorn. She could quite understand how Mr Dinsmore wanted to shut himself away from the world and both she and her father had tried to get through to him that he shouldn't do that, but as yet they'd been unsuccessful.

'How long ago did your wife pass away?' Nathan asked quietly.

'Coming up for twelve months.'

'You'll have lots of memories in this place.'

'Can't bring myself to leave it.' Mr Dinsmore's voice cracked on the last word. 'Every time I step outside that door, it brings it all back. It reminds me that she's gone. My Sadie. My beautiful, temperamental Sadie.'

'A wild one, was she?'

'Oh, yes.' Mr Dinsmore chuckled and Morena heard Connor gurgle happily. She edged into the doorway to get a better view of the three males, all of them at different phases of their lives yet all bonding in the way men seemed to when they were left alone.

'My Sadie was one of a kind. Tough as nails and gorgeous to squeeze.' He looked up at Nathan. 'Probably shouldn't talk like that in front of the young fella here.'

'Talk any way you like. He doesn't understand you, just the tone of your voice.' Nathan was wrapping the blood-pressure cuff around Mr Dinsmore's arm. 'I take it you and Sadie had a brood of your own?'

'Seven, we had. Lots of grandchildren, too. The youngest one is about the same age as little Connor here.' Mr Dinsmore lapsed into reflection again and Nathan was able to get a good reading. 'She's missing it.' The words were said softly and once more the old man's voice broke. 'She's missing it all. The new baby. The changes in the town. The sunsets. Even the stupid new water restrictions. Not that she'd be against them. No, she always bucketed the bath and washing water onto her garden.' He sighed. 'She loved that garden.'

Nathan had packed the sphygmomanometer away and was once more sitting next to Mr Dinsmore, just listening.

'She's missing it.' This time, as he said the words, tears started to stream down his face. Holding Connor out, Nathan was forced to take him while the other man fumbled about for a handkerchief. Nathan held the baby out at arm's length, Connor gurgling at having someone new to look at.

Hold him, Morena willed silently but Nathan looked very uncomfortable. When he finally looked over to the doorway and saw her standing there, he beckoned her over by angling his head. Quietly, she walked over and took her son off his hands. Mr Dinsmore seemed embarrassed that she was back and witnessing his moment of distress so he quickly blew his nose before excusing himself and shuffling from the room.

'I'll put Mr Dinsmore on my house-call roster from now on. I'll see him every second day and the district nurse can do the days in between. If he doesn't want to leave this house at the moment, that's fine.'

Morena nodded. 'We should have done that before now but he always insisted he was fine to come to the clinic.'

'I'm sure he didn't want to be any bother and, besides, sometimes we don't realise what's really going on until we stumble across the real reason. Mr Dinsmore probably felt he *was* fine to come to the clinic but lately, with the anniversary of his wife's death approaching, he's been needing to feel closer to her than before. Realising you've lived a whole year without someone brings unavoidable reflection and a whole list of what-ifs.'

While Nathan spoke, he walked to the sink and poured a glass of water, setting it on the table along with some white tablets. 'I'll also keep watch on Mr Dinsmore's depression.'

Morena nodded. 'BP elevated?'

'Yes. These tablets will do the trick for now, although I'd

like to change his medication as some hypertension medicines can bring on heavier bouts of depression so let's try lifting some of that off his shoulders.'

'Good thinking.' She was watching him closely, understanding a little bit better how he could relate to those on their patient list who had suffered loss, trauma and loneliness. It was because Nathan had been through all of that and probably more. He knew what they needed, whether it was someone to talk to, someone to laugh with or just someone to listen. So simple, yet so effective.

'What are you doing for dinner tonight?' she asked impulsively.

'Er…nothing. Why—is there something going on?'

'No. I just thought you might like to come over and have dinner with Connor and me. Nothing flash, just a basic meal although I promise not to purée your food.' She smiled but Nathan continued to stand there and look at her. 'That was supposed to be a joke. Obviously not that funny… But anyway, if you'd rather not, that's fine.'

'Of course he'll have dinner with you,' Mr Dinsmore said as he shuffled back into the room and gave Nathan a nudge. 'When a beautiful woman invites you around for dinner, especially if your only plan was to sit at home and eat in silence, you accept.'

Morena smiled at him. That sounded more like the Mr Dinsmore she remembered. 'You're welcome to come, too.'

'Aw, no, thank you, dear. I like to stay in at night now.'

'It's going to be a warm one and we're expecting a string of hot summery days so you make sure you put your air-conditioner on.'

'It's just me. I'm fine with a little fan,' he protested.

'You put your air-conditioner on.' Morena was serious but the underlying thread of love was evident in her tone. 'Drink lots of water, take your tablets…' she pointed to the tablets Nathan had put on the table '…and stay cool.'

'Still as bossy as ever.' Mr Dinsmore shook his head. 'So much like my Kaylee.'

'And Kaylee will want her dad to be cool this summer.'

'Right. Away with you both, then. You've got what you came for. Checked me out. Satisfied your curiosity. Now leave me alone.'

'I want to see those tablets swallowed, please.'

Huffing and puffing with annoyance, he did as he was told then looked at Nathan. 'I hope I'm seeing you from now on. This one's too bossy for my liking.'

Nathan nodded. 'I'll be around to see you.' He held out his hand and shook the other man's warmly. 'Have a relaxing evening. Put on Sadie's favourite music and relive happy memories.'

Mr Dinsmore squeezed Nathan's hand with manly gratitude. 'I'm glad to be sad if it means I can think about my Sadie.'

Morena's throat tightened over at his words and tears pricked behind her eyes. She rubbed her hand lovingly over Connor's back, needing his nearness. As though he understood, he snuggled in once more. Picking up the baby bag, leaving her medical bag to Nathan, she said her own goodbye and headed out.

'Have dinner with her,' Mr Dinsmore said to Nathan as she left. 'It's fine for an old man like me to be alone and pine away for days he'll never get back again but you—you're a young man. Go. Give the memories of your own past a rest for the night.'

'How did you…?' Nathan stopped.

'I can see it in your eyes, mate. Hear it in your voice. Those who have loved and lost can recognise the same pain in others.' He pointed in the direction Morena had just gone and Nathan wasn't sure whether he was telling him to get out or whether he was referring to Morena's own trauma. He received his answer a moment later. 'It's not easy for that one to reach out.'

'Right. Thanks.' Nathan collected the medical bag. 'See you tomorrow, Mr Dinsmore.'

'Looking forward to it, boy.'

Neither Nathan nor Morena spoke as she drove away, not until she pulled up outside the clinic. 'Here you are, then.' She kept the engine running.

'What? We're eating dinner at the clinic?'

'Oh! Sorry. I didn't realise you'd accepted my offer. Oh. OK, then.' A little flustered, she put the car into reverse.

'No. It's my fault. I should have been clearer.' Why was he suddenly feeling so nervous?

'Are you sure? You don't have to if you don't want to. It was just a spur-of-the-moment thing.'

Nathan looked at her. 'Don't you want me to?'

'No!'

'Uh… OK, then.' Disappointment flooded him.

'No, I mean, I *do* want you to,' she rushed on, desperate to get them both reading from the same page. 'I'd love it if you came over. It's usually just Connor and I in the evenings and he sleeps for the early part of it.'

'And wakes when you're trying to sleep.'

Morena laughed, putting the car into motion. 'Exactly. Sometimes it's gets a bit…well…'

'Lonely?'

'Yes.' She nodded. 'But there's always paperwork.'

'Thank goodness for paperwork.'

'The saviour of many a dull evening.' She pulled into the driveway of the block of apartments she lived in and pressed the remote-control button for her garage door.

'We live for paperwork,' Nathan said as she brought the car to a halt and switched off the engine, plunging them into silence.

Morena laughed nervously and shifted in her seat. 'We must lead very sad lives, compared to others.'

'Sad but safe.'

In the darkness of the garage, with the summer evening light shining in, his face was all angles and planes, but she could hear the emotion in his voice. It wrenched at her heart, made her yearn for him to be happy once more. Although still a stranger in many ways, Morena knew enough about Nathan to know he was a good man deep down inside and it pained her to see him hurting in this way. On impulse she reached out and took his hand in hers.

'What happened, Nathan? What happened to make you so terribly sad?'

CHAPTER FOUR

NATHAN looked down at his hands in hers. Who was this woman to be asking him such questions? He didn't even speak about his past with his parents…he couldn't. It was still too painful yet somehow Morena had picked up on that pain, had realised there was deep-seated hurt within him. He wasn't sure why he was so surprised because although he didn't know much about her, he, too, had witnessed a glimpse of the pain she'd been through.

'Why do you want to know?' He kept his voice controlled as he spoke.

'I'm trying to understand, trying to see if there's anything I can do to help.'

'You can't.'

She was a little taken aback at the vehemence of his words and withdrew her hands as though burnt. Her actions made Nathan feel like a bully. He hadn't meant to sound so fierce and wanted to apologise at once. Morena had been hurt before by a callous man and he hadn't meant to treat her in the same way. Still, he watched as she regrouped and tried again. 'I'm not meaning to pry—'

'Really? Could have fooled me.'

'It's just that if I have some understanding of what happened then perhaps we can sort things out better at work.'

'Meaning?'

'I know you're not fond of pregnant women or young babies and I'm guessing this has something to do with your past. If you're unnerved in some way, we can make sure you don't have these patients scheduled to see you. Your relationships with the patients are highly important and I know you're one hundred per cent professional, but there's also no reason to cause you extra pain by putting you in a situation where you're uncomfortable.'

'You would do that?' He was very surprised.

'Why not? We're a family practice, Nathan—emphasis on the *family* part. That doesn't just pertain to our patients but to our staff as well.' She watched his face, noticing his features relax and become less stern, more like the Nathan she was coming to know. 'Besides,' she said, trying to lighten the atmosphere, 'I promised my mother I'd do what I could to make you so comfortable at the clinic that you wouldn't leave at the end of your contract.'

He didn't make any comment to that, didn't smile, didn't move. He simply sat there, totally astounded at the level of caring this woman exuded. She'd chosen the most perfect profession for her personality. She was a nurturer through and through and he'd had evidence of that during his short time at her practice with the way she honestly cared for everyone she saw—even troublesome patients like Mrs Henderson! She may not get along well with them but she definitely *cared*.

She was a good person, a person who'd been knocked down and badly hurt on a deeply emotional level. The whole town knew about it, the whole town discussed it and still she went on, day after day in the face of the gossips, in the face of the sceptics and in the face of those people who were right beside her, supporting her all the way.

'Look, I know you think I'm sticking my nose in where it doesn't belong, but I hope we can be…well…friends.'

'Friends?' Why did the word sound so foreign to him? Nathan let out a breath and unclipped his seat belt.

'Yeah. You know. We talk, we laugh, we sometimes hang out.'

'Perhaps even eat dinner?'

'Exactly. As I said, I don't get a lot of adult company in the evenings and…we seem to get along well enough. So why not be friends?'

'And you won't ask too many probing questions?'

Morena laughed at that. 'I can't promise anything but seriously, Nathan, if you're uncomfortable at work, let me know. The last thing I want to do is cause you more sadness.'

'You'll cause me hunger pains if we sit here for much longer.'

'Good point.' Morena unbuckled her seat belt and turned to look at her son, who'd been sitting in the back, his teething ring in his mouth, listening to their conversation and quite content. When he saw his mother looking at him, though, his legs started to kick and his arms waved about in the air, his happy gurgling noises making Morena smile.

'Come on, then, my sunshiny man. Let's get you inside.' They headed inside, Morena bending to pick up a few things here and there, mainly Connor's toys, so Nathan wouldn't step on them. It was strange having someone else in her tiny apartment and a *man* at that.

She shook her head as she hooked Connor into his baby exerciser. It hadn't been her plan to get involved with anyone, especially another doctor and one who was currently working in her medical practice, but there was just something about him. Sally would say that it was a connection of their hearts but, then, Sally was a hopeless romantic who had found her own happily ever after and wanted Morena to find hers.

'What is that thing?' Nathan asked, snapping Morena out

of her reverie. 'It looks like an ancient torture device.' He pointed to the suspended harness Connor was in.

'It's an exerciser.'

Nathan smiled for the first time in hours. 'Yep. That's what they called ancient torture equipment—exercisers.'

Morena laughed, glad at the lightened atmosphere that seemed to surround them. 'I hook him into this harness, which supports his torso, the bit between his legs helps keep him in place and then…' She lifted the bar that ran across the top of the harness. 'I hook him onto the clamp here, which as you can see has a large spring attached to the doorway, and Connor can kick his legs, jump up and down and get all his energy out.'

'Is that good for a colicky baby? Jumping?'

'He hasn't been fed.'

'But I thought you'd fed him at Mr Dinsmore's?'

'Did you see me feed him?'

'Come to think of it, no.' He waggled a finger at her. 'You used the baby as an excuse to get into the house and then left us alone to talk.'

'Gee, and here I was thinking that you were smart. Bit of a worry if you're just cottoning on now.'

'Funny,' he replied with a droll smile. 'You're very funny.'

'I have my moments.' Connor was now jumping so high he was contracting the spring and the laughter and gurgling that came from him was enough to warm Morena's heart and brush away the day's cobwebs. 'That's it, my darling. Have some fun.' She turned to face Nathan. 'Right. Now that he's taken care of for the next half an hour, how about we get some dinner ready?'

'Hang on a minute. What's this *we* part? I thought you'd invited me around for dinner.'

'I have and you've accepted, which means you get to help out.'

'Some date you are.'

'This isn't a date, Nathan. It's two colleagues having dinner to help combat the loneliness that comes from living alone.'

'But you don't live alone,' he felt compelled to point out.

'True, and while my son is most definitely the apple of my eye, he's not too big on talking. Even the most devoted mother needs some adult conversation every now and then.'

'Should we cover his ears?'

Morena took a moment to understand what he was saying and laughed. 'Not *that* sort of adult conversation.'

'Darn.'

With the atmosphere one of jovial communication, Nathan set about preparing a salad while Morena put some potatoes in the oven to bake. Next she quickly defrosted two steaks and set them on the grill plate to sear.

'I'm sorry I don't have a nice bottle of wine to go with this but—'

'That's the price you pay for being spontaneous or perhaps you didn't really expect me to accept?'

'Well…I'd hoped you would and although the invitation was spontaneous, I had planned on asking you over at some point.'

'To welcome me to the neighbourhood?'

'Something like that.'

Nathan sat on the stool at the bench and looked at his surroundings. Many photos of Connor during the different stages of his young life lined the walls, the most recent being the baby with a Santa hat on, eating a shining piece of Christmas paper.

'I see Connor celebrated his first Christmas the way babies usually do.' Nathan pointed to the photograph.

'Eating the paper? Yes. That, and I think he played more with the boxes his toys came in.' Morena took a breath and then plunged in. 'What about your children? Did they do that at their first Christmas?' She knew she was treading on egg-shells—well, eggshells littered around broken glass and land-mines but still she had to ask.

Nathan's face paled but he didn't break her gaze. She'd said she wanted to be his friend and he hadn't had a friend—someone who was interested in *him*—for a very long time. This was an important moment in his life, the moment when he opened up and actually mentioned his past. 'My son didn't get to see Christmas. He…' He took a deep breath and let it out slowly. 'He didn't get to see anything. He died before he was born.'

Morena swallowed the pity that swamped her. 'How long ago was that?' Her tone was gentle and filled with empathy.

'Ten years ago.'

She raised her eyebrows, having thought his pain was quite recent, not that that made any difference as far as the amount of grieving was concerned. 'I take it you hold yourself respon-sible for his death?'

'His death. My wife's death.' Nathan shrugged and Morena let out her breath slowly. She'd opened this can of worms, she'd all but pushed him to tell her, and now that he had she wasn't at all sure what to say next.

'Nathan. I'm…' She stopped and shook her head.

'The steaks smell like they're done. I'll go and wash my hands.'

'Bathroom's on your right,' she said, as he turned his back to her and walked away. Morena closed her eyes and bit her lip. The scent of the steaks filled the air, Connor's laughter surrounded her. All about were the signs of life but they meant nothing when grief encompassed someone so completely. He'd been grieving for ten years and was still highly affected by whatever had happened to take the lives of his family. No wonder he'd been able to bond with Mr Dinsmore and other patients but…*ten years*? Morena opened her eyes as realisation dawned on her. Nathan wasn't still grieving. Instead, he was living off the guilt their deaths had brought him. It wasn't at all healthy but she doubted he'd appreciate her saying so.

'Right.' He rubbed his hands together as he came back. 'Are we ready to eat?' Morena decided to take her cue from him and nodded brightly. 'Good, because I'm actually quite hungry.'

'Excellent. Well, if you could take the salad and the cutlery over to the table…' She pointed to the dining table which was beside her lounge. 'Oh, and if you want to put on some music, feel free. I think I have a jazz CD in there at the moment but pick anything you like.'

'You like jazz?' He seemed surprised.

'Sure. That a problem?'

'No. No. Just hadn't picked you as the jazzy type.'

'Is that a compliment or an insult?' She chuckled.

'Neither.' A moment later the strains of her favourite jazz singer filled the air, although Nathan quickly turned the sound down.

'Sorry. Connor and I were dancing yesterday evening so I had it louder than usual.'

'It's fine.' He continued to look through her music collection. 'Kind of a cosy set-up you have here. Actually, it's about the same size as my apartment.'

'Well, we don't need anything big, just being Connor and myself.' She smiled at her baby, who was starting to tire a little but still jumping quite happily. 'You don't take up too much room, do you, darling?'

'He will as he gets bigger,' Nathan felt compelled to point out.

Morena merely shrugged. 'We'll cross that bridge when we come to it. I've learnt the hard way not to borrow trouble.'

'Did you live here with your husband?' Morena almost dropped the steak she was transferring to the plate at his question. When she looked at him, he shrugged his shoulders.

'I thought we were being open and honest with each other tonight. You've asked me personal questions. I just thought it was my turn.'

'Fair enough. No. Bruce and I lived at Encounter Bay.'

'That's just south of here, right?'

'Yes. It's like the next suburb over. We had a really nice house overlooking the ocean.'

'And you moved here?'

'It was necessary.'

'Why?'

Morena set the food on the table and went back to the fridge for a jug of water and two glasses. 'Hey, I thought it was my turn to ask a personal question,' she protested.

'You can have a free one when the inquisition switches back in my direction.'

She pretended to consider this as she sat down. 'Fair enough. The reason I sold the house was that I needed money. Bruce wanted out of everything so I needed to buy him out.'

She couldn't look at him as she spoke and Nathan picked up on her body language, which seemed to scream her inadequate and insecure feelings.

'Do your parents know?'

'No.' She looked up at him, a pleading look in her eyes. 'Please, don't tell them. They don't need to know. Not with Dad's health being what it is.'

'So your ex-husband not only didn't want to be a father but he wanted completely out of your life as well, right?'

'That about sums him up.' She gave a nervous laugh. 'Picked a good one to marry, didn't I?'

'I'm sure he led you to believe you were marrying someone very different.'

'How can you say that? You don't know him.'

'No. But I know his type. They need to have the latest of

everything, need to be seen to be a success, care far too much what the Joneses have and see money and the vast amounts they can procure as the most valuable commodity around.'

'My gosh. You *do* know him.'

'Told you.'

'You did.' Morena found herself smiling. 'Think you're so smart, don't you?'

'Don't need to think it. I *know* I am.'

Now she laughed and they started to eat. She could hear that Connor was starting to get tired and if she didn't take the opportunity to eat her food while it was hot, she'd be having a reheated dinner in about an hour's time once her son was settled.

'You mentioned before that you and your husband—'

'Ex,' she corrected him.

'Ex-husband.'

'Thank you.'

'Had bought the practice from your parents. I take it that means you had to buy him out?'

'Yes.'

'So now wouldn't be a good time to discuss the possibility of putting computers into the consulting rooms?'

'No.'

'I didn't think so.'

'Don't get me wrong, Nathan, I'd like nothing more than to bring the practice into the twenty-first century and computerise the place, but it just isn't possible. Not right now. I'm managing to keep my head above water and that's about all I have the brain power for at the moment.'

'I could take some extra duties off your shoulders if you like.'

'That's what you're supposed to be doing—in a medical capacity.'

'Sure, but I can help in other areas.'

'How?'

'I've been a practice manager before. I could help with the books, day-to-day upkeep, ordering, that sort of thing, or does Sally do all of that?'

'No. Sally's a people person, not a manager, and I'm a firm believer in that people should use the gifts they've been given to the best of their ability, rather than be burdened by things they don't like doing.'

'You're burdening yourself. Aren't you?' When she didn't reply he continued, 'I take it Bruce was the manager before he left?'

'Yes. He certainly had an aptitude for business. My dad used to do it but…'

'You don't want to ask him for help because he's supposed to be de-stressing not adding more to his plate.'

'Exactly.' Morena breathed out a sigh of relief, glad Nathan seemed to understand.

'So now you're forced to overburden yourself doing things you're not gifted at doing.'

'It's my job. I'm the owner of the practice.'

'And while I'm here it's not a burden you have to carry by yourself.'

She shook her head. 'Thanks, but I can't pay you anything extra.'

'I'm not asking for payment, Morena. Just call it part of my duties.'

'I couldn't do that.'

'Yes, you could.'

She was touched, so much so that she could feel tears begin to prick behind her eyes. It had been a long time since anyone had offered to do something nice for her and even though this was work related and not along personal lines, having Nathan help her out would be the biggest weight off her shoulders.

'And what happens when you leave at the end of your contract?'

Nathan frowned. 'Good point.' He thought for a second. 'All right, how about I teach you some little known tricks to help make the burden lighter for you to carry?'

Morena's heart sank. Not because of the offer to help but because it did seem as though he was definitely planning to leave at the end of his six months in Victor. She had no idea why she should want him to stay. She knew it was a six-month position but in her mind she'd hoped that whoever filled it might decide to stay on and make the position permanent. Now that she'd met Nathan, talked to him and even ogled him, she was more eager than ever in her wish that he might choose to stay at the end of the contract.

'What do you think?' He lifted his elbows onto the table and steepled his fingers together, looking at her intently. Morena was mesmerised by the way she could lose herself in those eyes. He was so incredibly good-looking that she was beginning to find it difficult when they were together like this not to read more into things. For instance, right now she could swear that they were having one conversation with their words and a completely different one with their bodies. His eyes seemed to be conveying the fact that he found her interesting and attractive and that he definitely wanted to get to know her better on a more intimate level.

But she knew that was ridiculous. It *was* ridiculous, right?

She sucked in a deep breath and slowly let it out in a desperate attempt to control her overactive heartbeat. She may indeed by attracted to Nathan but that didn't necessarily mean a thing. She'd been attracted to many men over the years. True, she'd only married one of them and it wasn't as though Nathan was proposing marriage—he was only trying to help her out of a jam. Wasn't he? Had she misread the signals again? She'd believed everything Bruce had told her, even when he had been busy making *her* feel guilty for *his* infidelities. She narrowed her eyes and angled her head to the side, giving Nathan a thoughtful look.

'Why do you want to help?' She knew she sounded suspicious but she couldn't help it. After what Bruce had done to her, she'd at last learnt to be cautious. 'You don't have to do this, Nathan,' she added, hoping she didn't sound too bad now.

'I think you need help. I know how to do the work.' He shrugged. 'The choice seems obvious. Besides, I'm offering and…' he straightened and leaned back in his chair, his eyes still intent on hers '…I'd like to help. We can do it together. At least that way you won't be pounding your head against a brick wall. I'm good with numbers, I always have been.' He gave a nonchalant shrug and smiled. 'It's my gift. Or you could simply call it the help of a friend.'

'Friend.' She said the word so softly he wasn't sure he'd heard correctly. 'And numbers are your gift, eh?'

'Yes.'

'One of many. Making persuasive arguments might be considered another.'

'My mother would agree with you.'

'Would she, now? Does that mean you were a charmer in your childhood?'

'Possibly.'

'So do you come from a large family?'

He shook his head. 'Only child.' He held up his hand to stop her next lot of questions. 'And before you ask, my father died three years ago—nothing tragic, just in his sleep. Sitting down in his favourite chair, listening to his favourite radio programme, a nice cup of tea on the table beside him and my mother sitting in her chair next to him, knitting.'

'And your mum?'

'She's over in England, visiting her sister and having a terrific time.'

'Sounds great. She has a love of life?'

'She does at that.' Nathan frowned a little and as tonight seemed to be one for honest communication, he ventured, 'I envy her in many ways.'

'Most people would.' Morena finished her dinner, hearing Connor beginning to niggle a little. 'We all just sit in our houses, eating dinner night after night, work day after day and never really venture out of our comfort zones. I admire people who do.'

'You want to travel?'

'Of course, but not right now. It's certainly not the right time now, but one day I will. It's not a huge yearning or anything, don't get me wrong. I love my job, I love being close to my parents, to the people I've known for most of my life, working in the community where I was raised and feeling as though I'm giving something back. I find myself quite… content with where I am but there are so many places I'd love to see.'

'Such as?'

'Venice.'

'Top of the list?'

'Yes. I love sunrises. I'd love to see the sun wake Venice up. Or the sunrise over the Grand Canyon. The pyramids. Uluru.' She smiled dreamily as she cleared the table and Nathan wondered if she knew how delightfully lovely she looked. So simple and elegant even though she was still dressed in her workclothes of a lightweight cotton dress that flowed around her ankles. Most of her hair had come loose from her ponytail but it just added to the ethereal effect surrounding her.

Nathan continued to watch her as she moved around, stacking the plates next to the sink, still chatting about differ-

ent places she'd like to see. He was listening but he was mesmerised by the way she almost glided around so smoothly, so
flawlessly. He couldn't remember ever seeing a woman move
with such grace. The fabric and shape of her dress was
feminine and cut so as to entice the imagination, and his was
being enticed. The lines of her arms were smooth, her neck
was sculpted to perfection and as she came to remove their
glasses, leaning across, almost brushing close to him, her
subtle scent surrounded him, and he exhaled slowly.

She didn't seem to realise the effect she was having on him
and continued doing the mindless household chores, only
needing the occasional murmur from him to keep the conversation going.

'Are you listening to anything I've said?' Morena finally
asked, standing before him with her hands on her hips.

'Huh? What?' Nathan sat up straighter in his chair. 'Of
course I was listening. You were telling me how Mr Dinsmore's
daughter Kaylee had been over to study art in Paris before she
returned to Australia to get married and have her family.'

'Mmm. Very lucky.'

'I was listening,' he promised, and stood, gathering the final
few things from the table, bringing them into the kitchen and
putting them on the bench. It was then he realised his mistake.
Morena's kitchen was as small as his own and with the two
of them in there and Connor jumping slowly in the doorway,
it made for an even more confined space.

The main problem was that usually when he found himself
in situations like this, soft and intimate—which this one definitely was—his first instinct was to run a mile as fast as he could.
But here and now…he was more than happy to feel that faint
prickle of awareness spread slowly over his body as he acknowledged the fact that he wanted very much to kiss Morena.

It was ridiculous. It *was* ridiculous, right?

His mind was in a whirl and for the first time in…well, a long time, he wasn't sure what his next move should be and that was a dangerous area to be in. Still, he found himself unable to move from where he stood just in front of Morena, who was trapped between himself and the bench.

Nathan looked down into her upturned face and saw the hint of uncertainty at what was happening between them, what was starting to grow and blossom. The seed had been planted when they'd first met, from the moment they'd looked at each other, from the moment they'd shaken hands and felt that frisson of awareness. Already it had grown and he knew it would soon blossom if they weren't careful. Then it would start to grow completely out of control and he knew neither of them needed that.

It didn't change the fact that the urge, the desire to kiss her was definitely there and as Morena's blue eyes dipped nervously to his mouth and back up to meet his gaze once more, he knew the desire was mounting in her as well.

Someone needed to break the moment but she wasn't at all sure she wanted to and even if she did, how did she do it? He was before her, standing so close she could feel the warmth radiating from his body, mingling with the scent which was now synonymous with him and would continue to remain so for ever. Did she want him to kiss her? She wasn't sure. Well, part of her was but the other part—the rational part—was sure she didn't.

Indecision was something Morena had dealt with in the past but ever since Bruce had left her in the lurch she'd had to learn how to make decisions and that was what she did now. She couldn't let him kiss her. It was wrong. It would only bring further complications but despite what arguments her rational mind put forward, the overwhelming desire to feel the pressure of his lips on hers was becoming too hard to fight.

Neither of them moved…until Connor's tired cry filled the air.

CHAPTER FIVE

AS THOUGH waking suddenly from a dream, Morena somehow managed to shift around Nathan, only realising belatedly that he'd moved back at the sound of her son. Cooing and murmuring softly to Connor, she unhooked him from his exercise bouncer and carried him, harness and all, into his bedroom. 'Won't be long,' she called over her shoulder.

What had she been thinking?

Morena set about on autopilot, getting Connor changed and ready for bed, her thoughts running wild. She'd been standing there, frozen with anticipation mixed with excitement staring up at Nathan, almost willing him to haul her into his arms and press his mouth to hers.

The question was why? Why should she be feeling this way? She'd vowed to be much more cautious before becoming involved with another man again. Hadn't Bruce shown her that men could be liars, that they never revealed their true selves? Although Nathan had professed to being honest tonight as they'd been talking and, indeed, he *had* opened up and told her some terrible things about his past, that didn't mean she should be willing him to kiss her!

'What's wrong with me?' she whispered to her son, who was still niggling, indicating he was ready to eat and then go to bed. 'I mean, I like him, Connor. I do. I really do, and perhaps that's part of the problem. But instead of liking him…you know…*that* way, I should be trying to help him instead. The man has been suffering from guilt for a whole decade and that's just not healthy, my son.' She lifted him into her arms and kissed his chubby cheeks. 'Don't you do that, all right? Don't ever let yourself get consumed by such a negative emotion. You can get consumed by love, I don't mind that, especially if it's for me.' She buried her head in his tummy and managed to get a tired giggle from him.

Sighing and feeling a little more in control, Morena carried her snuggling son back out from his room and stopped short when she found Nathan standing at her sink, his hands in dish-water as he finished off the washing-up.

'You didn't have to do that,' she instantly protested, depositing Connor in his highchair and slipping a clean bib over his head. She gave him a teething toy to chew before walking into the kitchen. Bruce had *never* done anything domestic and that included volunteering to do the dishes. He had preferred to pay someone else to do that, saying that no wife of his was going to do housework either.

'It was the least I could do after you'd cooked such an enjoyable meal. Besides…' he swished the water around once before pulling the plug '…they're all done now.'

'Oh. Well…thank you.'

'You're welcome.' It was there again, that smile behind his eyes, as if to say that he was pleased to be surprising her. 'I take it your husband wasn't big on the domestic side of things?'

'What are you? A mindreader?'

Nathan chuckled at that. 'It was just the look on your face when you saw me with my arms covered in suds.' He watched as Morena once more flitted around the small space, getting her son's evening meal ready. 'You shouldn't judge all men by your ex-husband's standards.'

Morena nodded. 'I guess. Old habits—and all that.'

'Yes.' Once more their eyes met and held and Nathan found himself experiencing that dangerous pull yet again. It was the reason he'd started doing the dishes in the first place, needing to keep himself busy so his mind didn't wander into the 'what-if' category. He wasn't even ready to accept the fact that he was attracted to the woman before him because if he did that, it would mean he was ready to move on and he knew he wasn't ready to move on at all.

She was so…untouched and fragile. It tapped into every one of his protective male instincts and he wanted to scoop her up and promise to keep her safe for ever. That thought alone was enough to break the link.

'I'd better go.'

'Why?'

Now it was his turn to be surprised by the question. 'Well…you need to get Connor settled and off to bed and no doubt you're tired.'

'Connor won't take long, he's very tired. Then we could talk some more.'

Nathan's mind ran through the appealing scenario. The two of them sitting on her lounge, facing each other and chatting quietly with jazz providing the perfect accompaniment in the background. It was far too appealing.

'I think it's better if I go.' He stepped towards the door.

'Do you need me to take you home? I can drive you.'

Why did she sound so eager? Did she want him to go?

'It's fine. My place isn't far from here. You've got Connor to deal with so I'll just…' he indicated the door behind him '…go.'

She had a child. Why hadn't she remembered that? Of course he wanted to get out of there. He was uncomfortable around babies because it brought back too many painful memories of what had happened in his past. Even if there *was* some underlying connection between them, it would all come to nothing because she was a mother.

'OK, then.' She forced a smile as she headed towards the door, Nathan a few steps in front of her. Once there, she leaned past him and unlocked the door, her shoulder accidentally brushing his. She gasped softly at the touch and murmured, 'Sorry.'

'It's all right. You didn't hurt me.'

Trying to control the flurry of buzzing tingles which were now zinging their way around her body, spreading to areas long dormant, Morena giggled nervously. She looked up at him and found that super-sexy smile on his lips, the one that had made her knees go weak from the first time she'd seen it. Why did he do that? One second he was all but pushing her away and the next he was making come-hither eyes at her.

She fumbled with the doorknob and locks, her fingers feeling like they were made of jelly.

'Let me help you,' he murmured, so close to her ear his breath fanned over her neck.

'It's fine,' she snapped a little too suddenly, and Nathan drew back. 'I've got it,' she offered more calmly. 'Here you go.'

She turned to look at him and if she'd thought they'd been close in the kitchen, it was nothing compared to how intimate they were right now. If she leaned up a little bit and he leaned down… Her heart was pounding wildly against her chest, she was positive he could hear it. Her breathing increased, coming out in audible little gasps. Nathan's eyes dipped down to look at her parted lips before meeting her gaze once more.

'Thanks again for dinner.' His voice was deep, sexy and husky, and it didn't help her equilibrium one little bit.

'You're welcome,' she breathed. Step back. She needed to

step back, to put some distance between the two of them. If he was going to leave, he should leave. If he was going to stay he should… She cut her thoughts off. This was wrong. This was all wrong.

Finding strength from somewhere, Morena shifted, bumping into the bookshelf and wincing as the corner dug into her hip. She didn't care. He needed to leave before all her strength, all her resistance left her and she threw herself into his arms.

Resistance was plummeting to an all-time low and he was positive that neither of them knew what to do about it. It was the strangest sensation he'd ever felt. So close, so intimate and yet so wrong, he wasn't at all sure what to do. His mind searched for another time when he'd felt this way so he could recall what he had done back then—but nothing was coming up. Was he in uncharted waters? That wasn't a good thing. He'd prided himself on always being in control, always being able to handle every situation, but most of all having his emotions firmly under wraps. So why was the need to hold Morena in his arms so overwhelmingly powerful?

'We should do it again some time.'

'Pardon?' Nathan's eyebrows hit his hairline. Could she read his thoughts? Did she *want* him to hold her?

'Dinner. We should do it again some time.'

'Dinner.' Relief flooded through him. 'Yes. Dinner again would be great.'

'I'll even make sure I have a nice bottle of local wine next time.'

He nodded and smiled, edging his way towards the open door. 'Sounds great. I haven't had much of an opportunity to visit the local wineries. New job. Boss keeps me busy,' he explained, tongue in cheek, and Morena's answering smile was full and bright—and it went right to his solar plexus.

They'd managed to break one intimate moment. Nathan

had no desire to create another one and continued to instruct his feet to move. 'OK, then. I'll see you tomorrow.'

'You will.' Connor started fussing and Morena sighed. Commitments. She had a commitment to her son and right now it was the thud back to earth she needed.

'You'd better go.' He indicated her impatient son.

'Yeah. Bye.' With a resigned shrug Morena slowly closed the door. Leaning against it for a moment, she listened through Connor's cries for any sign of Nathan's footsteps walking away but couldn't hear anything. Was he still outside her door? Lingering? Not wanting to leave, just as she hadn't wanted him to go?

Her gaze fell on her son. 'Oh, baby, I'm sorry.' She hurried into the kitchen and finished preparing his food before sitting down and feeding him. 'You're so tired honey. I know. I'm a silly mummy who's just reading something into nothing. And besides,' she continued as he gobbled his food, 'I've got you and I don't need any other man…especially one that isn't planning to make Victor Harbor his home. We're better off just the two of us, right?'

Connor's answer was to bring up his wind.

An hour later, with Connor settled, Morena paced around her small apartment, picking up the toys, fluffing the cushions on the lounge and generally trying not to remember how it had felt to have Nathan there. They'd had such a good time that it was difficult to get him out of her thoughts.

She went to the kitchen to make herself a soothing cup of herbal tea, hoping that would help settle her mind, but standing there in the kitchen only reminded her of Nathan being there, helping her prepare the food, doing the dishes and then being close…so close. She closed her eyes and sighed at the memory. It was the strangest sensation and one she hadn't felt before—that tug, that pull, that overwhelming need to simply give in to temptation and go for it!

Yet she wasn't that type of person. She wasn't a woman to throw caution to the wind and let the moment take her where it may. She'd been that woman—before she'd met Bruce—but now she was a person who was careful, thoughtful and…frightened of being hurt again.

When her phone rang, Morena jumped, clutching her hand to her chest as she stared at the inanimate object. Usually, she would pick up the phone the instant it shrilled to life, just in case it woke Connor, but tonight it rang three times before she picked it up, her heart pounding wildly in case it was Nathan. Would he be ringing her? Why would he ring her? What would she say?

'Hello?'

'Hello, darling. How did things go today?' It was her mother and Morena sighed with a mixture of relief and disappointment.

'Fine.' She took her tea over to the lounge and sat down, tucking her feet beneath her.

'You don't sound fine.'

'I'm just tired. As usual.'

'And how was Nathan today?'

'Nathan? Oh, he was fine, too,' she said, wondering why her voice sounded so high-pitched and totally unnatural.

'That's good. I hope you're talking the town up, showing him the best spots. Have you taken him out to Granite Island? The Bluff? What about that cute little miniature village? It's a pity it isn't whale-watching season. I think Nathan would like to see the whales.'

'Really? And how do you know that, Mum?'

'Well when he came around for a barbeque on the weekend, he said how much he enjoyed scuba-diving and marine life in general. We told him to go to the whale centre but at this time of year, with it still being school holidays, there are children everywhere and I remember you saying that he wasn't good around young kids.'

Morena listened to her mother talk, forgetting they'd invited Nathan around on the weekend. She'd been a little put out that they hadn't asked her as well but she guessed they had a right to get to know Nathan themselves—especially if her mother intended to convince him to stay in Victor Harbor longer than he was contracted to.

'I haven't had much of an opportunity to show him around, but when we drive out to the different house calls I make sure I point out anything of interest.'

'You should invite him to the Bluff this weekend. It's perfect weather to go walking out there. You'll have the sun shining and the wind blowing—that way you don't get too hot or too cold. We'll look after Connor so you don't need to worry about carrying him in the backpack up and down those wild rocks. Nathan will love it.'

'That he might, Mum, but I don't think so.'

'Why not? Morena, you do want him to stay don't you? He's so good with your father's patients—even your *father* thinks so.'

'That's great, Mum.' Morena closed her eyes and sighed.

'What is it?' Joyce's tone changed to one of maternal concern.

'I like him, Mum.'

'We all do, dear.'

'No. I *like* him.'

'Ooh!' Joyce squeaked. 'Oh. Well…OK. So you like him. That's more of a reason to get him to stick around. Right?'

'Oh, Mum, I don't know,' she wailed, and slumped down across the lounge, burying her face in the cushion for a moment.

'A little sudden.'

'Well, I certainly wasn't looking for anything. It's just happened.'

'What's just happened? Has something happened?'

'No. Nothing…physical. I mean, he hasn't kissed me or anything.'

'But you want him to.'

'Yes.' The word was a sigh of longing. 'And that's ridiculous enough in itself. Mum, what am I going to do?'

'About what, dear?'

Morena frowned. 'Haven't you been listening? About Nathan?'

'Why do you need to do something about it? Why not let nature take its course? After all, he's been here for, what? Almost a week and a half? He has more than five and a half months left and I'm sure we can sort out a relationship for the two of you in that time.'

'*Mum!*'

Joyce chuckled and apologised. 'I'm sorry, darling, but I don't see what the problem is.'

'What if I get hurt again? That's probably the biggest question that comes to mind. What if Nathan and I decide to get involved while he's here and then we argue and fight and things turn sour, or else he turns out to be not the man I thought he was or things go great and then he still leaves at the end of his contract? There are so many variables. *Too many* variables and I simply can't deal with it all right now.'

'You can't judge every man by Bruce's standards, Morena,' her mother said quite seriously. 'Bruce was wrong for you. That doesn't mean Nathan is as well. I'll admit that in the beginning Bruce had us all fooled—not just you, but you definitely got hurt the most.'

'He did hurt me,' she admitted softly. 'He tore my heart out, ripped it into tiny little pieces and then blew them away, letting them float to wherever—he didn't care.'

'Aw, sweetheart.' Joyce could hear the pain and anguish in her daughter's voice. 'Do you want me to come round?'

'No. It's all right. It's just…after everything, after the way he treated me, the way he stripped away my confidence, my self-worth, my love…' She broke off as her voice cracked on a sob. 'I was weak, I was gullible and I was a fool. Am I any good now? What if Nathan doesn't want me either? What if I'm damaged goods? What if no man could ever love me again, Mum? What then?' Tears started to trickle down her cheeks but she couldn't be bothered to wipe them away.

'Morena Camden, you listen to me,' her mother said firmly. 'Are you listening?'

'Yes.'

'You are not weak, you are not gullible and you are not a fool. You are a survivor and you've proved that to everyone since Bruce left—and good riddance to him, I have to say. You can't focus on the past, you know that. You have Connor to think of and a life to live.' Joyce's tone had gentled a little now. 'So go live it, my darling.'

'You're right. I know you're right and most of the time I feel as though I'm in control, but then there are times like now when I dwell too much on things and I end up going from one bad thought to another, ending up like a puppy chasing its own tail.'

'So what are you going to do about Nathan?'

Morena sat up and wiped at her eyes. 'I'm going to be his friend.'

'Friends. That's good, and it appears you could both use one.'

Morena thought about what Nathan had confessed to her earlier on, about his past, about his family. He was lonely and he was hurting as well. Yes. They would be friends. Friendship she could handle for now. They were going to be good friends as well, not just work colleagues but real friends. 'Friends.' The word was said with a firm and solid resolve.

* * *

Nathan almost slept through his alarm the next morning. He'd tossed and turned for most of the night, unable to sleep and unable to control his thoughts. His head had been filled with visions of Lila and the way she'd looked when he'd found her dead in their home. The news that his unborn child had been male. The way his parents had tried to help him, the way he'd shunned everyone around him and taken off—needing to get away, needing space.

And through this haze of thought came a ray of sunshine. A ray of light, of hope…and it was in the vision of Morena. Her strawberry blonde hair all messy as she rushed here and there, her blue eyes alive with life but still exhausted from lack of sleep. Her smile shining brightly at him, encouraging him and probing gently to get him to open up and talk about the past.

He didn't speak to anyone about Lila. Not to his parents, not to his friends—no one. He'd moved around, never keeping still for the past ten years because every time he started to get settled, he'd be haunted with what he'd let happen to his wife. She'd been alone when she shouldn't have been. If only he'd gone straight home. If only…

Nathan threw back the covers, determined not to think about it any more. Work was the answer. Work had always been the answer. He could immerse himself in a new practice, be distracted from his thoughts by meeting new people. It was how he'd always coped in the past and this time would be no different. The fact that Morena had happened to get under his skin, to ask him those probing and hurtful questions—and the fact that he'd actually answered her rather than just brushing her aside—none of it mattered. He was there to work. To do his job. And at the end of his contract, he would leave.

His alarm buzzed again and he forced himself to get out

of bed. As Morena usually ran late in the mornings, it wouldn't do for both of them to turn up late.

When he arrived at the clinic, he was astonished to find Morena in her consulting room, reading through a stack of medical files.

'You're here!' She was wearing a white top with thin straps, showing off her sun-kissed skin. Her hair was back in its usual ponytail but today it wasn't as messy as usual and it was held in place by a clip.

'Where else would I be?' she asked, glancing up at him but continuing to work.

'Well…it's just that you're often late.'

'And you thought that was the way it was going to continue?'

Nathan frowned. 'Er…I…uh…don't know. Is something wrong?'

'No. Just have a lot to get through today.' She gave him an indulgent smile but continued working. 'Will you be ready to leave for the retirement village round in about fifteen minutes?'

'Of course.' He left her to it, deciding not to worry about Morena and her moods. If she said there was nothing wrong, then he would believe her. When Sally came in, both doctors were ready to leave.

'Connor had a good sleep last night, then?' Sally sat down behind the desk and punched in the code to take the phones off the message-machine.

'He did.'

'Hallelujah! I hope that means you slept well, too?'

'Well…' Morena shrugged, feeling self-conscious about having this conversation in front of Nathan. It was true that Connor, for the first time ever, had slept through the night. Unfortunately, Morena had been teased with dreams of

Nathan and she hadn't wanted to be. She'd spent half the night tossing and turning with visions of herself and Nathan locked in a tight embrace, and the other half going to check on Connor to make sure he really was still breathing and wondering why he wasn't waking up.

'Oh, dear. Anyway, go and get the retirement village round done and perhaps you can have a sleep this afternoon when Connor has his nap,' Sally suggested.

'Sounds like a plan. Ready to go, Nathan?'

'Absolutely.' He smiled at Sally before heading out to Morena's car, unable to stop himself from ogling Morena's legs. She wore a short skirt today and was showing a good deal of leg and he swallowed over the roughness in his throat as he appreciated the shapely contours, trying to get his mind to focus. 'I take it you didn't have a good night, then?'

'No.' She put her bag in the back of the car and climbed behind the wheel.

'Me neither.'

She closed her door and looked at him. 'Really?'

'Perhaps it was something we ate?'

'Perhaps…although I wasn't actually sick. Just couldn't settle my mind down.' They were going to be friends. *Just* friends!

'Hmm.' Nathan nodded but didn't say anything else. Morena drove them to the retirement village where most of the residents were able to fend for themselves, with nurses to monitor them daily and help out when they couldn't cope. They went and spoke to all the residents, spending quite a bit of time with every single person. He realised that Morena treated every patient as though they were very special to her, and he became aware as they told stories about when she had been younger that they were—each and every one of them.

'That's the trouble with growing up and working in the

same place,' she said as they left one unit and went to the next. 'Because they know me, they feel they all need to tell you a Morena story.'

Nathan chuckled. 'Do you hear me complaining? I'm learning so much about you, although I didn't have you pegged to be captain of the softball team—more like captain of the debating team.'

She wasn't sure whether to be insulted or not and stopped where she was, glaring at him. 'Are you saying I'm good at arguing?'

'Yes.'

'Or is it just that I never shut up?'

Nathan thought for a moment. 'Both, actually.'

'Well, thank you *very* much, Dr Young.'

'You're welcome.' He started walking again and Morena quickly caught up, loving the way they shared this uninhibited banter. It was something she'd never really experienced with a man before and she was liking it a lot. 'So who's next?'

'You're enjoying this, aren't you? And I'm not talking about the stories about me.'

'Yes, I am. The elderly are often shoved aside by the younger generation and I often wonder why. They have so much wisdom and knowledge. Combine that with open honesty and laughter and you have a winning combination as far as I'm concerned. I have to say that this facility is fantastic. It has everything they need.'

'It *is* good. My father was instrumental in getting it set up like this and it's been open about fifteen years now.'

'Fantastic.'

'Hold on a moment.' Morena stopped again and handed him the paperwork she was carrying. 'Won't be long.' She pointed to the amenities behind her. 'Too many cups of tea, I'm afraid.'

'Not used to socialising so much?'

'Oh, I socialise enough but I don't usually drink so much tea. It's your fault, you know.'

'My fault? How so?'

'They're all eager and anxious to charm you—well, the ladies at any rate, the men just want to get your opinion on everything they're into, whether it be cars, computers or horticulture. I just get to tag along for the ride and bask in your glory.'

Nathan laughed and shooed her away. It wasn't long before she returned and as she went to relieve him of the papers, he said softly, 'I'll carry them.' He'd insisted on carrying the medical bag when they'd arrived and now had the papers tucked into the crook of his arm.

'Oh. Thanks. I see chivalry's not dead?'

Nathan laughed at that. 'They're papers, Morena. Hardly heavy, and me carrying them is hardly worth being called chivalrous, but don't let me stop you.'

'Still, it's the thought and the gesture that counts so I shall indeed count them and I thank you, kind sir.'

'You're very welcome, fair maiden.'

Morena couldn't believe how light and happy she felt as they walked along. There was a smile on her face and a spring her in step and she had such a feeling of contentment that it would be the most natural thing in the world for her to link her arm with Nathan's as they strolled along in the January sunshine. The feeling that she'd known him for a lot longer than she had again washed over her and instead of ignoring or trying to justify the fact, she decided to simply enjoy it.

He made her feel all girly and feminine and to that end she'd worn one of her favourite floral skirts today, which came to just above her knees and showed a lot of leg. She'd teamed it with a white cotton top and flat shoes, adding a dainty gold anklet she hadn't worn since she'd been at university. It had been a gift from her cousin and today she wore it with the confidence of days gone by.

Of course, when she'd dressed that morning, she'd told herself time and time again that it wasn't for Nathan, even though she'd been fooling herself. As she hadn't been able to sleep, she'd had the opportunity to spend a bit more time on her appearance, something she hadn't done since before Bruce had left. Bruce, of course, had expected his wife to look pristine and elegant and because of that she had a wardrobe full of beautiful clothes, clothes she now hardly ever wore. Since Connor's birth, she'd just thrown on whatever had been clean and ironed—sometimes forgoing the ironed part due to lack of time.

But today she'd wanted to look nice—nice not only for herself but for Nathan as well. For some reason she *wanted* him to see her as an intelligent and desirable woman and at least now she had the sense to admit it to herself.

It didn't mean that anything was going to happen between herself and Nathan but she accepted the fact that he made her feel feminine, that he made her feel intelligent and that he made her feel desirable, and she hadn't felt that in such a very long time. She'd made the decision when Bruce had left that she wasn't going to let any men into her life on a permanent basis. She had Connor to look after and a practice to run and that left no time for short-lived romances. A crush? Perhaps. A mild flirtation? Why not? She was her own boss and that's the way it was going to stay.

'Mrs Doonan. Here we are, number 12.' Nathan checked the papers he was holding.

'That's right. She's had a cold for the past week. My father saw her last week and said she was doing all right, but I'd still like to check her.'

'The nursing staff say she's doing all right.'

'Which is good, but I think it's best we check her nevertheless.'

'It's what we're here for.'

'Yes, it is.' She knocked on the door. 'Mrs Doonan? It's Morena.'

Nathan stood beside her as they waited for a response and once more her fresh scent surrounded him. It was the scent that had haunted him all night and one he was eager to smell when he'd gone to work that morning. It wasn't right and he knew it.

'Hello?' The unsure voice drifted from behind the door.

'Mrs Doonan? It's Morena. Can you open the door?'

Nathan took a step back, determined to regain his senses. What was it about this woman that made him so aware of her? He could feel himself being drawn to her and that wasn't right. He didn't want to feel anything but guilt...yet guilt and bright sunshine didn't usually mix. He needed distance. Nathan took another step back and felt his ankle twist on the edge of the path.

'Whoa.' Like a scene from a movie, he could see himself falling backwards in slow motion, the medical bag dropping to the ground with a thud, his arms flailing helplessly to the side as he grabbed at the air, papers flying off in all directions. Morena looked at him with stunned surprise, then reached out a hand to him—but it was all too late. He landed with a thump in Mrs Doonan's garden, surrounded by squashed flowers.

'Oh, my dear, are you all right?' Mrs Doonan appeared at the door in time to witness his humiliation.

'I'm fine. It's fine.' He saw other people, gardeners, nursing staff, come running over. 'I'm fine. Really.' To prove it he hauled himself to his feet without any help from Morena, who was now holding out both hands. 'There. See? Fine. Nothing broken—except my dignity, of course.'

Morena started to chuckle as she bent to gather up the papers and he was glad of the reprieve from her attention. It gave him time to get his embarrassment under control. The staff, after making sure he was really all right, went back to their duties.

Mrs Doonan took the bag and papers from Morena and beckoned them inside, putting Morena's things down by the chair. 'I'll go put the kettle on,' she said, and hurried to the kitchen. 'We can all have a nice cup of tea.'

'Ah. Tea.' Morena's voice was soft. 'The old-fashioned cure for…well…everything!' Morena smiled at Nathan, then noticed that as he put pressure on his foot he winced.

'Here. Let me help you.' Instantly, she put her arm around his waist and lifted his arm around her shoulder so he could lean on her.

'I'm all right. *Really.*' The last thing he needed was Morena's body pressed up against his in such an intimate way.

'Oh, hush. You're the patient, so do as your doctor says.'

'Morena!' He sounded as though he was in pain.

'What?' She looked up at him and froze. Her heart started beating in double time, her mouth went dry and her entire body was flooded with anticipatory tingles.

There, in his rich brown eyes, she saw the full-blown emotion of what she'd received only a glimpse of last night.

There was pain, yes, but it wasn't from his fall because mixed with the pain was…desire. Pure, unadulterated desire, and it was so powerful he'd been unable to hide it.

It was only then she realised they were now practically in each other's arms. Her breathing increased as her hand, which was at his waist, now registered the firmness of his body, the taut muscles beneath his shirt tantalising her sense of touch.

'Uh…' All logical thought fled from her mind as she continued to gaze into his eyes, mesmerised by what she saw there. It hadn't been her imagination, she hadn't been seeing things or reading the signals incorrectly.

Nathan desired her—and she reciprocated the emotion one hundred per cent.

CHAPTER SIX

'Mmm.' He breathed in deeply. 'You smell so good.' The words were said in a rushed whisper, his breath fanning over her face causing goose bumps and his words igniting a flame throughout her body.

'You're not too bad yourself,' she countered gently.

'What is this thing between us?' His voice was husky, the desire still very evident.

'I don't know.'

'How do you take your tea, Dr Young?' Mrs Doonan came into the room and both Morena and Nathan looked at the floor, focusing on the task at hand. They made it over to a chair and Nathan reluctantly took his arm from Morena's shoulders as he lowered himself into it.

'Black. Thank you.'

'No sugar?'

'No. Thank you.'

'Ah, just like Morena.' Mrs Doonan came over to stand beside Morena. 'How is he?'

'*He*,' Nathan said, 'is just fine. Embarrassed but fine.'

'I'll check him out, Mrs Doonan. Don't you worry.' Morena bent down to take a closer look at Nathan's foot.

'Good. Oh, there's the kettle boiled.' She rushed back into the kitchen, leaving the two doctors alone.

'Morena, this isn't necessary.' He twitched when she touched his ankle. His pride was injured, nothing else. Why couldn't she just let him be? His reaction had nothing to do with any injuries from tripping over. He needed to get her to stop touching him. 'You're hurting me,' he finally said, and lifted his foot from her hands.

'Well, I would have thought, as a doctor, you'd know that a little manipulation *would* hurt.'

'I'm not talking about my ankle,' he ground out between clenched teeth, and she jolted as she realised what he *was* referring to.

'Oh.' She stepped away, unable to speak for a moment. 'Uh…' She swallowed. 'You've definitely sprained it but if you rest it and strap it, it should be fine.' It took a moment for her brain to reboot and she realised that despite whatever it was that existed between the two of them, she still needed to treat Nathan's injury. She took a bandage from the bag.

'Thanks for the consult. I'll bandage it when we return to the nurse's office.'

'No. I'll do it now. The sooner it has more stability the better, and as far as the attraction we feel goes—well, we'll just have to ignore it until I'm finished.' She reached for his ankle. Both of them were silent while she went about her task, both of them trying not to react to the nearness of the other.

Just as she finished, Mrs Doonan handed her a frozen packet of peas.

'Here you go, dear. Use that for an icepack.'

'You don't have a proper icepack?' Morena said.

'Ha. This is what I used when my kids were little. It worked then. It will work now.' Morena wrapped the peas in a cloth and put it on Nathan's ankle, which was elevated on a small stool.

'Of course, there was the time…' Mrs Doonan chuckled '…when I was in hospital, having my gallbladder removed, when my husband used the wrong bag of peas. Never lived that one down.' She headed back into the kitchen and returned a few moments later, carrying a tea tray. Morena left her tea to cool a little and checked Mrs Doonan's blood pressure, making sure she was keeping her fluids up and resting.

'Oh, yes, dear. I'm feeling much better than when I saw your father last week.'

'Excellent. That's what I like to hear.'

'Yoo-hoo!' There was a knock at Mrs Doonan's door and two other ladies came in. 'Sorry, love. We couldn't wait to see the new handsome doctor. Mavis was all but raving about him and was on the phone to us the instant you left her place. Ooh, will you look at him, Dorothy? He's a handsome one, isn't he?'

Morena smiled. 'Nathan, meet Mrs Cobb and Mrs Reynolds.'

Nathan removed the peas and rose to his feet, showing no signs of wincing as he did so, and shook hands with both women.

'Oh, don't be so formal, Morena.' She fluttered her eyelashes at Nathan. 'You can call me Edna.'

'Pleased to meet you, Edna.'

'And I'm Dorothy,' the other woman quickly interjected.

'A pleasure.' Nathan's charm was having an amazing effect on the three women. 'Please, come and sit down.'

'No.' Mrs Doonan was on her feet. 'It's not fair. He's come to visit me and you'll just have to wait your turn.'

'Oh, but if you let us stay,' Dorothy wheedled, 'you can come with him when he comes to see us. I have some fresh scones in the oven,' she said temptingly. 'They'll be ready in about ten minutes so drink up your tea.'

'But I'm supposed to be having a check-up,' Mrs Doonan kept protesting.

'Oh, Morena can do that, can't you, dear?' Dorothy had sat as close to Nathan as possible without actually sitting *on* him, and Morena couldn't help the twitching of her lips.

'He's a right gorgeous one, Morena. Please, keep him around. I promise to keep every appointment I make and always have scones in the oven when you visit,' Dorothy continued.

Nathan's smile was wide and bright, indicating he loved every moment of the attention he was receiving. The good thing was, she could also use it in her favour.

'He's due to leave at the end of June, Dorothy, but if you want to twist his arm and encourage him to stay, please, do so. *I* have no objections.'

'Ah…you want him all to yourself,' Edna piped up. 'Typical of you young girls. Always keeping the sexy ones for yourselves.'

Morena wasn't sure whether to be outraged or to laugh. She chose the latter and took a cup of tea from the tray. Mrs Doonan—who insisted Nathan call her Gina—played hostess and indeed when it was time to move on to Dorothy's, they all trooped over there to eat fresh scones with jam and cream. Morena stayed at the back of the harem as they walked. Not only was it safer back there but she could monitor the way Nathan was walking to assess just how much damage he'd done to his ankle. His limp was slight but still there and she had the feeling he was trying to play down the extent of the pain. Whether it was for her benefit or so the other ladies didn't fuss and worry about him, she wasn't sure.

'See?' he said softly to Morena as he stood at the door, letting the women precede him. 'It's not that bad.'

So he'd been aware of her appraisal. 'Sprung?'

'You're either too obvious or I'm just too brilliant.'

'No doubt you think it's the latter.'

'No doubt.' He grinned at her as they went inside. Once the scones had been served and praised, Morena stood.

'Let's get your check-up done, Dorothy.'

'No. Nathan has to give me my check-up,' she said, starting to unbutton her blouse.

'I still need to be in the room.' Morena shook her head at the audacity of these women.

'Oh, I have no concerns that Nathan won't be an absolute gentleman. We'll be fine, won't we?' She smiled warmly at him, fluttering her eyelashes once more.

'I meant I need to be there to protect *Nathan*, not you, Dorothy.' They all laughed. 'Besides, it's the law.'

'Oh…all right, then.' She stood and headed into the bedroom and Morena followed with the medical bag, Nathan behind her. He took Dorothy's blood pressure and listened to her heart while Morena stood there and handed him the instruments he needed. He checked Dorothy's eyes and ears and looked into her throat.

'Any complaints?'

'Only that my heartbeat might have increased.'

'You've been having palpitations?' Nathan was instantly concerned.

'I think she means because you're close to her,' Morena clarified in a stage whisper, and when Nathan looked at his patient, he saw the twinkle in the older woman's eye.

'You're an incorrigible flirt, Mrs Cobb.'

'I've had three husbands, you know.'

'Really?' Nathan handed the stethoscope back to Morena.

'Outlived them all, I have. Strong as an ox.'

'Excellent. That's what we doctors like to hear, isn't it, Morena?'

'Oh, absolutely.' They returned to the other two impatient women and continued their extensive morning tea.

'This is a picture of my twin granddaughters, River and Inara.'

'Those are their names?' Nathan asked.

'Oh, yes. My daughter always liked different names. And that's their dog—Jayne.'

'The dog's called Jayne?' Nathan wanted to get it right. Now that one woman had shown him photographs, the others brought out small albums they apparently carried everywhere with them. He looked to Morena for help but she simply smiled and he returned his attention to the photographs thrust before him.

At Edna's house, they had fresh cake and homemade lemonade.

'It's my family's secret recipe,' she whispered to Nathan after he'd complimented her on the refreshing drink. 'I'd be happy to give it to you, if you'd like.'

Morena just sat back and shook her head and when he glanced over in her direction, she winked at him, letting him know he was well and truly on his own.

'You tiger, you,' she said when they were safe in her car, heading back to the clinic.

'What?'

'Oh, you have the gift all right. The gift of charm, the gift of flattering and flirting. One day, though, one of them is going to take you seriously and haul you to the altar.'

Nathan chuckled. 'You won't come and rescue me?'

'Ha! It'll be your own doing. You're as bad as the lot of them.'

'What? It's all harmless.'

'And that's why you like it,' she said. 'Because it's safe and harmless.'

'And a bit of fun.'

'And a bit of fun,' she repeated.

'Do you want me to stop?'

'Good heavens, no. I've never seen the three of them so animated before and *all* of them promising to take better care of themselves at one tiny hint from you. No, you have a gift, Nathan, and while you're here I intend to exploit it.'

'You mercenary thing, you.'

Morena laughed as she pulled the car up outside the rear of the clinic. 'You'd better believe it.' Both of them entered the practice, still laughing at some of the morning's events, and met her father. 'Dad!' Morena stepped forward and kissed his cheek. 'How are you feeling today?'

'Not as peppy as you two. How were the residents at the retirement village?'

'All eager to meet Nathan—and flirt with him,' Morena supplied.

'Ah.' Edward nodded as he shook Nathan's hand. 'Excellent. That'll bring a bit of renewed life to the place.'

'And gossip. All of them will be getting ready for next week's visit,' Morena said as she went into her consultation room and took the bag and papers from Nathan.

'Mrs Doonan's cold?'

'Cleared up.'

'Good. Good. And what about Mrs Reynolds?'

Morena and Nathan gave Edward a debrief on the patients they'd seen that morning, her father nodding with satisfaction at the report.

The tinkle of the bell over the doorway sounded and Edward nodded. 'That will be my first patient. We're not booked too heavily this afternoon, Nathan, so if you wanted some time to recuperate from your morning's outing, I can handle the cases this afternoon.'

Morena was instantly alert, concerned that her father was wanting to take on too much. 'Nathan doesn't mind,' she said quickly. 'And if he stays, you can get through the clinic more quickly and both finish early.'

'You could take Nathan out to the Bluff or Granite Island.

Show him around a bit of the town.' What was it with her parents wanting her to show Nathan around? It was obvious that her parents had discussed their daughter and the newest member of the clinic and had come to the conclusion that they should become better acquainted. Not that Morena didn't want that either but she didn't want Nathan to think that every member of her family was throwing themselves at him. She half expected him to turn the offer down and was astounded when he did the opposite.

'Sounds like a good plan,' Nathan said, and could feel the daggers Morena was glaring into his back. 'I've hardly seen anything of Victor Harbor since my arrival.'

'Morena can definitely show you the best spots,' Edward suggested. 'She has this afternoon off to spend with Connor.'

What? Was her father trying to increase his workload or play matchmaker? She glared at him instead. 'What if—?' she began but Nathan interjected.

'Why don't I go and take a look at the list? If it's not as full as you say, Edward, then I'd love it if Morena showed me around a bit.'

'I'll have Connor,' she said pointedly.

Nathan nodded. 'Great.' He and Edward walked from the room, leaving Morena stunned. Last Monday, he hadn't wanted to have a bar of her because she had a child. Now he wasn't bothered about spending time with him. She frowned. Perhaps Nathan had decided that now she knew about his past, he could open up to her, spend time with her, become her friend. Whatever was happening, it was confusing, to say the least.

An hour later, after they'd both gone to their respective homes to change and have lunch, Morena pulled her car into a car park near the causeway to Granite Island. Her mother had offered to keep Connor for the afternoon while Morena and

Nathan spent time together, but Morena wasn't having any of it. Besides, she and Nathan were going to be friends and as her friend, he would need to come to terms with the fact that she had a son and that she enjoyed spending as much time with him as she could. At the moment Connor was in the back, oozing gorgeousness as his tummy was full, his nappy was clean and he'd had a great morning sleep. She looked at him in her rear-view mirror and smiled.

'What?' Nathan asked, seeing her smile.

'My son. He's so yummy.' With that, she opened the door and came around to the passenger side to get him out.

'So what's the plan?' Nathan asked, coming to stand beside her. 'What historic sight of Victor Harbor are you planning to show me?'

'I can show you a few from here,' she said, and straightened up for a moment. 'We've already driven past the Newland Memorial Church but over there…' she pointed '…is the Old Customs and Station Master's House. It was built in 1866 and is now the National Trust Museum. Just over there…' she changed her direction slightly '…is the Whale Centre, which all the schoolchildren love to visit.' She turned once more. 'And there is the tourist information centre, where you can get a lot of information on Victor Harbor and the rest of the Fleurieu Peninsula. Then there's the Granite Island historic horse tram, which takes thousands of tourists across the historic causeway out to historic Granite Island every month.'

'A very…historical place.'

'Historical or hysterical?' she asked, with a smile and returned to her mission of extracting her son from his car seat.

'You came to Adelaide from Sydney? Is that right?'

'Newcastle. Close enough.'

'Novocastrians wouldn't like to hear you say that. Mr Dinsmore's daughter, Kaylee, lives in Newcastle and they're very particular about not being known as an outer suburb of Sydney—given that it's a two-hour drive between the cities.'

'Point taken. Are you planning on carrying Connor around all afternoon?'

'All afternoon? What about your ankle?'

'It's fine. The exercise will be just what it needs.'

'Liar, and we both know it.'

'Seriously, my ankle's much better,' he insisted, and she held up her hands, indicating she wasn't going to argue. He was a grown man *and* a doctor and if he said it was better, then it was better.

'OK. So you're happy to spend a whole afternoon with us?'

'You did volunteer to show me around,' he pointed out, as she drew Connor from the car.

'Volunteer? I don't remember that. More like you and my Dad coerced me, although I'm still not sure why.'

'Why what?' He watched as she walked around to the boot and opened it, taking out a baby backpack.

'Why you wanted to spend the afternoon with us,' she answered, putting the carrier down and taking out the baby bag before closing the boot.

'Why wouldn't I?'

Morena straightened and blew a piece of hair from her face. 'Because you freaked out when you discovered I had a child.'

'Ah.' Nathan nodded and followed her as she headed for a shady tree so she could get set up. 'I did. You're right.'

'I'm not complaining. I think it's great that you're willing to be around Connor, especially with what you've been through and the guilt you've heaped on yourself over the past decade. That's not easy to recover from, and I also know it's not something you simply shrug off overnight.'

'Hold on a minute.' He watched as she took a blanket from the bag and placed it on the ground before putting Connor down. 'Where do you get off saying I've been heaping guilt on myself for the past ten years? You know nothing about it.'

Morena wasn't put off by his attitude. She'd half expected it but she'd also expected that this would be something they would argue over. Despite the attraction they felt for each other, the baggage he was still carrying around after ten years was something she wasn't willing to take on board—*should* anything come of this attraction.

'That's right. I only know what you've told me but I quickly saw that you're not still grieving for your wife and unborn child, Nathan, you're feeling guilty instead.'

'It was my fault. Their deaths were my fault. I have a right to feel guilty.'

'Hmm.' Morena turned her attention to setting the backpack up, then picked Connor up and put him in the backpack, securing him.

'What? That's it? *Hmm* is all you're going to say?'

She folded the blanket and put it away before carrying Connor in the backpack to the park bench and sitting down, swatting a few flies away before slipping her arms into the straps and securing the harness around her waist. 'What else do you want me to say, Nathan? That you're allowed to waste your life wallowing in guilt? Because it's not. Grief is one thing, guilt is another.'

'And you know this how, Dr Freud?'

'Because Bruce was an expert at heaping guilt onto me.' If Nathan wanted to know about her marriage, she'd tell him. 'To hear him tell it, *I* was the reason our marriage failed. If *I* had been more desirable, he wouldn't have had to look elsewhere. If *I* had been a doctor with more grandiose ideas, he wouldn't have required more of a challenge in his professional life. If *I* hadn't fallen pregnant, if *I* hadn't flatly refused to have an abortion, he wouldn't have had to leave. That was the guilt he heaped on me and a whole lot more. I felt inadequate in every part of my life, in everything I did. *He* did that. It was Bruce who made me feel that way, but I *let* him, Nathan. I let him walk all over me, I let his gibes, his narky comments get to me. I borrowed his guilt, I took it on board and he let me. He heaped it on and then put sprinkles and a cherry on top. I spent the first six months after he left beating myself up and wishing I'd done things differently. He undermined my confidence, cut me down, piece by piece, little by little, until I was left with nothing...*feeling* like nothing, and swimming in a cesspool of guilt.' Her voice broke and she stopped, taking a few deep breaths to get herself under control.

'Yes, it still hurts,' she continued a moment later. 'Yes, I have to live with the memory of those words every day for the rest of my life and no doubt I could have done things differently—but it wouldn't have mattered because it *wasn't* my fault. It takes two to tango and Bruce was just as responsible for the breakdown of our relationship. I've since realised he was also too selfish, too self-centred and too immature to accept that.'

'So what changed?'

'Connor. Connor changed me. I'm less tolerant of people trampling on me. I'm a mother and my first duty is to protect my son, to raise him in a loving and caring environment where he can grow with confidence into a wonderful young man. I don't have time for guilt. It eats away at you, Nathan, and it will continue to eat away at you if you let it.'

'And you think I've been letting it?'

'Yes.'

'Know me that well?'

'No, but the fact that you don't like being around pregnant women, that you're uncomfortable around children shows me you've let it get to you way beyond reason.'

Nathan shook his head. He didn't need this. He hadn't asked for it but he also knew deep down that she was right. He didn't want to acknowledge it—wasn't ready to acknowledge it—not yet. 'That is your opinion of me?'

'No.' She picked up the baby bag and put it over her shoulder. It was time for truth—for both of them—and she took a deep breath before plunging in. 'My opinion is that you're an amazing man, with so much to give, so much to share, and I'm not talking about your qualifications or the practice here. Both of us feel…whatever it is between us and that's OK. It's OK that we're attracted to each other but it also doesn't mean anything if we're not prepared to take a step away from our past and move into the future. I like you, Nathan. I like what I've seen so far and I believe I can help you, give you support as you do whatever it is you need to do, but I can't do it for you.'

With that she pulled her hat onto her head and started walking towards the six-hundred-and-thirty-two metre causeway that led to Granite Island. Nathan wasn't sure for a moment whether or not he wanted to follow. The woman was infuriating and yet he'd opted to spend his afternoon with her. Why? He wasn't too sure. He only knew that after that moment they'd shared back at Mrs Doonan's place, when her body had been pressed against his, he wanted more. More of being able to touch her, more of being so close her scent filled his senses, and more of the opportunity to perhaps kiss her. The thought had kept him awake half the night and with it had come extra guilt for the memory of his wife.

Guilt. Morena was right that he lived his life by it. It was how it had been for so long that he wasn't sure he was able to change. She was also right that no one else could change it for him. Hurrying after her, he caught up with a few long strides.

'Check Connor's hat is on properly for me, please,' she said, and Nathan followed the instruction, his fingers brushing the soft, sweet cheeks of Morena's little boy. He was a cutie, that much was certain, and that one light touch brought with it a glimmer of hope.

'In position and shading him nicely,' he reported, pulling an old cap from his back pocket and putting it on.

Morena looked at him. 'Like that ratty thing is going to stop you from getting sunburnt.'

'Keeps the sun off my head and my face.'

'Sure, but your ears are really going to cop it. I'll give you some sunscreen when we get over to the other side.'

He nodded and they walked in silence for a minute, swatting flies here and there, though the sea breeze was enough to keep them to a minimum.

'Are you all right?' she asked softly.

'All right?'

She looked up at him. 'After what I just said, I'm surprised you still want to talk to me.'

Nathan shrugged. 'I'm fine.'

'Fine. Right.' She rolled her eyes.

'What now?' He spread his arms wide.

'My mother always said that "fine" stands for "finally, I'm not emotional".'

'Meaning that I'm bottling my feelings or brushing them aside?'

'Yep. Suppressing the emotion.'

'What if someone really is fine?'

'Then they usually use another word to describe the way they're feeling. They might say "good" or "great".'

'Right. I'll do well to remember that.'

'So…?'

'So…what?'

'So how are you after our conversation? Are you really OK with it or are you…*fine*?'

Nathan thought carefully before replying. 'I'm... *fine*. That doesn't mean I didn't listen to what you had to say. I did, and I also appreciate you sharing what you did.'

'OK.' Morena looked over at him as they walked over the uneven causeway towards the island.

Nathan looked across and smiled at her. 'OK,' he repeated, then surprised her by first taking the baby bag from her and then holding her hand, lacing their fingers tightly together. 'Let's have an enjoyable afternoon.'

'Yes.' Morena accepted the flood of excitement that tingled through her body at his touch. Nathan was holding her hand! 'Yes. It would be a shame not to enjoy this... *fine* weather we're having.'

Nathan's answer was simply to smile.

CHAPTER SEVEN

'It's beautiful here,' he said as they leaned on the rail of the causeway and watched the boats sail across the water in front of them. 'Very relaxing.'

'That's how I feel.' Morena checked her son, who was now sleeping in the backpack, which Nathan was carrying. After they'd walked across the causeway and then started on the one-and-a-half-kilometre walk around the island, Nathan had insisted on taking the backpack from her.

'Chivalry,' was all he'd said, and had refused to argue with her.

'Is he asleep?'

'Yes. Sitting there, doing nothing has tired him out.'

Nathan laughed. 'I know how he feels.'

'Tired?'

'Mellow.'

'Good.' He'd held her hand for most of the time they'd been walking but parts of the circular Kaiki track needed to be accomplished in single file and Morena had thought that once he'd dropped her hand, he wouldn't make the effort to hold it again, but she'd been proved wrong. Nathan had admired the low vegetation, Morena telling him the names of the different shrubs that were alongside the track. They'd stopped to read the historical facts about the island from both the white man's and the aboriginal points of view.

Now they were leaning on the rail, side by side, their arms touching. Warmth radiated through her body but in a comfortable way, not the flash of zings she'd experienced on other occasions. On the blue water between them and the mainland, sailing boats were out. Their sails were colourful, the boats leaving white wakes as they zipped along, the occupants obviously enjoying themselves. Nathan felt at peace for those few moments, just staring out to sea, watching those boats go by and wishing he could be on one.

'How do you get any work done? I mean, with this sort of inducement to get outdoors and relax, it must be hard to focus some days.'

'It is.'

'You know, the practice I worked at in Perth was situated ten minutes from the beach but we were always so flat out that I rarely got time to swim or surf.'

'That's a shame. It's important to recharge your batteries. It's the reason we all get one half-day per week off. It's necessary and that way we don't get burnt out.'

'And here I am having two half-days off this week.'

'You slacker.' They both laughed then Morena sighed. 'Although this is very pleasant, it's also quite hot and I don't want Connor out in the sun for too much longer.'

'Good idea. Shall we start walking back?'

'Well…I thought you might like to take the horse-drawn tram back. Perhaps give your ankle a rest.'

'My ankle is…*fine.*'

'What? It's better or it's not emotional any more?'

Nathan grinned and shook his head. 'Let's go catch the tram, Dr Camden.' As they walked towards the tram stop, Morena pointed out a few other landmarks.

'There's a fairy penguin colony here on the island and at night you can come and watch them as they go from the sea into their burrows for the evening.'

'Really?'

'Absolutely.'

'We should do that some time.'

Morena was happy with the suggestion, with the fact that Nathan seemed comfortable to spend more of his leisure time with her. 'We will.' While they waited for the tram, they walked to the kiosk and had ice creams, Connor waking up in time for the tram ride back.

'Not that he'll remember it,' Morena said as they sat up the top of the double-decker wooden tram, which was open to the weather, her son in her arms.

'It's just like a miniature London bus,' Nathan remarked.

'Except it's not red, is made of wood, is drawn by a Clydesdale horse and is a tram, not a bus but, yeah, apart from that, just like it,' she couldn't resist teasing.

Nathan laughed and rolled his eyes. 'Are you always this pedantic?'

'Uh…yeah.'

'Hmm. Remind me to watch out for that in future.'

In future? What did that mean? Was he thinking of staying here for longer than six months? She pushed the thought aside, not wanting anything to spoil the time they were having. It was as though the rest of the world had been put on pause simply so they could enjoy being with each other. He was even taking small steps with Connor and not looking at her son as though he were the carrier of the plague.

When the tram ride was over, Nathan climbed down the steps, carrying the backpack, but as the steps were quite steep, it was a little tricky for Morena to hold onto Connor as well as the handrail and navigate her way down safely.

'Here. Let me take him.' Nathan's words were gentle as he put the backpack and bag down before holding out his hands. Morena looked at him, wanting him to know she knew how big and important this was, but said nothing as she handed her son carefully down to him. Nathan didn't hold him close but didn't hold him out at arm's length either, merely held him for a half a minute so she could get down safely. Morena took her son back and in silence they headed back to her car.

'It was a terrific afternoon,' Nathan remarked as she secured Connor into his car seat.

'It was.'

Although they didn't talk on the drive back to his apartment, it was comfortable and again Morena realised that she had never felt this way about another man. It made her aware of how rare her growing feelings for Nathan really were. As she stopped outside his place, he unbuckled his seat belt and turned to face her.

'Thanks.'

'My pleasure.'

He didn't move and for a heart-stopping moment Morena wondered if he was actually going to kiss her. Her pulse increased and she was very glad to be sitting down so she didn't fall down. The atmosphere around them started to increase with unsaid thoughts and feelings, and eventually Nathan took her hand in his.

'I'd...I'd like to do this again, Morena. If that's all right.'

'Spend time together?'

'Yes.'

'I'd love to.'

'I mean, perhaps without Connor?'

Morena's heart plummeted and she tried not to let her expression change. 'He's part of me, Nathan. I know there's this thing between us but when it comes to crunch time, you can't have me without Connor. We're a package deal.'

'I'm not discounting that.' He dropped her hand and raked his through his hair in obvious agitation.

'Besides, you'll get to spend Saturday and Sunday with me at the hospital, not this weekend but the next.'

'Oh, super fun times there,' he said with a hint of sarcasm. 'It's not that I'm denying Connor's existence, Morena, it's just that usually when a man and woman date, they don't do it with offspring hanging around.'

'Hanging around?'

'That came out wrong.'

'Yeah.'

'When you're with Connor you're…distracted, conscious of him, of his needs. That's perfectly fine. You're his mother. It's necessary. I accept that. All I'm asking is for an evening where the two of us can go out to dinner. You know—do the date thing.'

'You're asking me out on a date?'

'And doing a very bad job of it, it seems.'

'Oh.'

'And?' he prompted when it appeared she wasn't going to say anything else.

Nathan wanted to *date* her? A rush of emotions swamped her, the like of which she hadn't felt since eighth grade and Stuart Petrofsky had asked her to the end-of-year dance. 'Uh…that would be…nice.'

'Nice? That's almost as bad as *fine*.' Nathan raised his eyebrows as he spoke, his lips starting to twitch into a smile.

Morena laughed. 'It is, isn't it? What I meant to say was I would be delighted.'

'Much better. We'll fix up a time and place later— whenever it suits your parents or whoever's going to babysit Connor.'

'OK.'

Then, before she could say another word, he picked up her hand once more and pressed a kiss to it. 'I'll see you tomorrow.'

'OK. See you then.'

With tatty cap in hand, he climbed from the car and headed up the path towards his apartment. Morena put the car into gear and headed off on the short drive to her own place. She forced herself not to think of Nathan until she'd bathed Connor and set him jumping in his exerciser. She forced herself not to think of the meal they'd shared together and how lovely it had been to have a handsome man round to dinner. She forced herself not to think of Nathan as she fed Connor and put him to bed—but it was all for naught.

The man continued to infiltrate her thoughts and was her constant companion as she went about her evening. With Connor finally asleep, she looked at the clock and sighed. 'Eight-thirty.' She didn't feel like watching television and she knew there was no way she would be able to settle her mind to a book.

Pacing around the apartment, she knew she needed to talk to someone, but who?

There was Sally. They'd been good friends since school and she could tell her anything, but Sally also worked with Nathan and, quite frankly, Morena could do without those little sneaky looks she knew Sally wouldn't be able to control every time Nathan and Morena were in the same room together. No. She would confide in Sally later, but not now.

'So who?' she sighed, and then snapped her fingers as the answer came to her. 'Kaylee.' It was half an hour later in Newcastle but she knew Kaylee was a night owl and would definitely be up. Dialling the number, it wasn't long before she was pouring out the story to her friend, who was almost as excited as herself by the time she'd finished.

'Wow. I can't believe it. And you've known him *how* long?'

'About ten days. It's ridiculous, Kaylee. I know it, I feel it, but I can't help it. I feel as though I've known him *for ever*, which is why this is spinning me out so much.'

'It's just so…good.'

'That it may be, but what do I do? I can't stop thinking about the man and last night I was tossing and turning, unable to get him out of my head. On top of that, it was the first night that Connor slept through.'

'Bummer.'

'You're telling me. I just can't take another night when I don't sleep because some man I hardly know is so vibrant I can almost touch him.' She breathed in deeply. 'I can still smell him, too, and it's *so* nice.'

'Then why are you fighting it?'

'Because I don't know anything about him. Because I've been hurt badly before. Because I have a child I need to care for. Because I have a practice that needs to be run.'

'Is this the same doctor you took around to see my dad?'

'Uh…yes.' Morena frowned. Ron Dinsmore must have said something to his daughter.

'My dad was really impressed with him and you know how he doesn't take to strangers.'

'Nathan's so amazing with most of our patients.'

'But he has baggage, right?'

'Who at our age doesn't have baggage, Kaylee?'

'Good point. So, anyway, what are you going to do about the amazing Dr Young? Apart from sending me a photo of him because I need to see what this one is like, especially as he has you all in a dither.'

'I am, aren't I?' She sighed. 'What do I do?'

'Let yourself go.'

'What?'

'Think about it, Morena. When was the last time you felt this way?'

'Uh…never.'

'Not even with Bruce?'

'Nope. Not like this. Bruce was more awe and fascination.'

'And with Nathan?'

'I feel like a fluttery girl again, wanting to dress nicely, wanting my hair to stay in place. I even wore make-up today.'

'Wow. He has got you in a spin.'

'So I just…what? Spin?'

'Why not? Acknowledge your feelings, validate them. Have you written your first name and his surname together yet to see what it looks like?'

'No!'

'Morena?' There was sternness in Kaylee's tone. 'You may not have done it but you've thought about it, right? All girls do. It's the girly way.'

'Oh, all right, I have thought about it.'

'Then do it. Write your feelings down if it helps you to understand what you're feeling, but above all don't try to ignore the way you feel. It's like chocolate. If you crave it and let yourself have a little bit, you're more likely not to eat the entire block in one sitting. If you ignore the craving, however—'

'You end up bingeing,' Morena finished. 'What if I become addicted?'

Kaylee laughed. 'I want to be maid of honour.'

'Kaylee!'

'Sorry. If you become addicted to him, I guess we're going to have another expensive phone conversation. Oh, why do I have to live so far away from you? Simon worked out the other day that the distance between Newcastle and Victor Harbor is like driving from the coast of Italy to England. Either way, it's way too far, in my opinion. Still, we'll be back visiting

Dad for the weekend in a couple of weeks. We'll catch up then, and I can even meet the man in person!'

The two women chatted for a bit longer but when Morena hung up she felt better. 'Validate my feelings,' she said, as she walked into her room and found an old journal she'd bought after Bruce had left but hadn't really had anything to write about. Now, with Nathan, it was a different story.

For the next few days, both Nathan and Morena were aware of each other at work but neither made any move to plan anything else, even though they both knew a date was in their near future. It was as though they simply enjoyed working together but didn't want to arouse suspicion with either Sally or their patients.

They hadn't made any plans for the weekend but Morena spent most of her Saturday thinking about him as she did her housework, cooking meals for the week and making sure she and Connor had clean clothes to wear. Once that was done, though, she felt as though the walls were closing in on her and gathering up her son and the paraphernalia that went with him, she headed out to the car.

Thoughts of stopping off at Nathan's apartment crossed her mind, of just turning up and asking him to accompany her to somewhere…*anywhere*…so long as they could spend the time together. Then again, as they hadn't planned anything, he might already be out and even if he wasn't, he might not want her intruding on his solitude.

Sighing, she turned the car towards the Bluff, deciding a nice walk was what both she and Connor needed to whisk away the cobwebs. As she drove slowly through town, she glimpsed Nathan walking down the street and quickly pulled over.

'Hi,' she said, getting out her car and heading towards him, a big smile on her face.

'Hi, yourself.' He came to stand in front of her, quite close really, and she had a difficult time stopping herself from closing her eyes and breathing in the hypnotic scent of him. 'Where are you headed?'

'To the Bluff.'

'Just you and Connor, or are you meeting friends there?'

'Nope. Just the two of us.' She jerked her thumb in the direction of her car. 'You could come. We'd love you to come. In fact, I was wondering whether I should have driven around to your place and invited you.'

'Really?' His smile was big and encouraging. 'I wouldn't have been home.' He indicated the street he had been walking down before shoving his hands into his khaki shorts, his cool cotton shirt unbuttoned enough at the top for her to glimpse a light smattering of chest hair. 'I was just getting some fresh air.' And trying not to think about her. It was the main reason he'd left his place, trying to get a new perspective on the way she was making him feel. Happy. Light. Free. It wasn't what he was used to.

'So…do you want to come?'

Nathan hesitated for a split second before nodding. 'Yeah.' He took her hand in his. 'Yes. I do.'

Morena's heart skipped a beat as he touched her, as the warmth of his skin enveloped hers, and even though the car was only but a few steps away, he didn't let go of her hand until the last possible moment when she walked around to the driver's side.

Nathan gurgled and waved to Connor, who gurgled and smiled back brightly. 'He's getting to know you,' Morena said as she drove the short distance to the Bluff.

'He's only seen me a few times.'

'He's a very smart little boy.'

'Takes after his mother,' Nathan pointed out.

'Thank you.' She parked the car in the Bluff car park and they both climbed out. When she took the backpack from the boot, Nathan immediately put it on.

'No argument.' He pointed up the steep incline of the walking track he could see from the car park. 'Carrying Connor on my back around this place is more of a workout than I can get at the gym.' He patted his flat abdominals. 'Gotta keep in shape.'

Morena's gaze dipped to where his hand was and allowed herself to openly admire what she saw. 'You're doing a fantastic job,' she eventually said, meeting his eyes once more and seeing the self-satisfied smile on his face. So he liked it when she looked at him, did he? Well, she'd be more than happy to oblige him in the future.

As they started up the steep path, Connor covered in toddler sunscreen and shaded by his hat, cooing happily in the backpack, Nathan asked for another history lesson.

'The Bluff…well, let me think.' Morena racked her brains while she concentrated on her footing, not wanting to slip or twist her ankle as they headed up the steps cut out of the rock. 'It was originally called Rosetta Head and was used as a whaling station. This was back in around 1830-something. I can't remember the exact year.'

Nathan tut-tutted. 'Do I need to get myself a different tour guide? Disgraceful.'

'OK. I'll find out for you and let you know if it's that important. I can tell you that it was declared a recreation reserve in 1938.'

'Well…all right, then. I guess I'll let you off the hook for not remembering the other date.'

Morena turned to face him as they reached the top of the first section, the wind whipping her hair around her face. 'Thank you. You're too kind.'

He smiled at her and then turned to look at the view, taking her hand in his as they stood there and looked out to sea, the clouds moving above them. There were other people on the walking track, they both knew that as there were other cars in the car park, but for the moment no one else was visible and it was as though it was the two of them, standing on the edge of the world—or was that the *top* of the world? It was certainly how Morena felt—on top of the world.

It was moments like this that helped her through her doubts about what was happening so rapidly between the two of them. When she paced around her apartment in the middle of the night, the thought of his hand in hers, the way he would smile that secret smile at her, the merest caress as he tucked the odd piece of hair behind her ear…those were the memories that helped push away the thoughts of what if?

What if he was like Bruce but was better at hiding it? What if she was putting herself out there to be hurt again? What if he didn't stay in Victor Harbor? What if she became so entangled with him that he broke her heart when he left? Bruce had left her and it had felt as though she'd died, it had been so difficult to breathe. Yet with Nathan…she'd never felt anything like this before and it was enough to make her realise that he had the power to hurt her far more than Bruce ever had.

No. She wouldn't think about that now. Now was the time for making wonderful memories and she intended to do just that.

The following week was a repeat of the one before, with them sometimes not seeing each other during clinic hours but enjoying the time they spent doing house calls. Ron Dinsmore was more receptive to their visits and had even been letting the district nurse into his house for the more regular check-ups.

'And Kaylee's coming this weekend,' he said brightly. 'She insisted on it.'

'I know. She told me over the phone last week,' Morena said, and knew she would have great delight in introducing her friend to Nathan. She also knew the main reason for Kaylee's visit was to be with her father as this coming weekend was the anniversary of Mrs Dinsmore's death. Neither Mr Dinsmore nor Kaylee had said anything to Morena about the real reason but they didn't have to. She knew…everyone knew…and where Morena had been concerned that Mr Dinsmore might lock himself away, the news of his daughter's planned arrival had been more than enough to brighten him up and put a bit of life back into his face—the way she'd remembered him.

'Coffee?' Nathan offered on Friday afternoon as Morena came into the kitchen.

'Tea, please. I've lived on coffee all day long. I think I need to start winding down.'

'Are you still feeding Connor?'

'Just two feeds a day. Morning and night, and don't wear that concerned doctor look with me. If you'll check the jar in the cupboard, there's decaffeinated coffee in there as well as tea.'

'Good.' He nodded his approval. 'How has Connor been sleeping?'

'Much better. It's as though he's finally got the hang of it.'

'And you?'

Although the question was quite innocent and very natural, given the circumstances, Morena felt her cheeks begin to grow warm as she met his eyes. 'I've managed two nights where it wasn't so disjointed.' And mainly because she'd given herself permission to dream about him, rather than fighting it. He was the first thing she thought about when she woke up and her last thought as she went to sleep—and it had been marvellous. 'What about you? No more sleepless nights?'

Nathan shrugged and brought her over her tea. 'Black, right?'

'Correct.' He sat down opposite her. 'So? Are you going to answer the question or avoid it?'

'Avoid it.'

'I see.'

'What do you see?'

'Well…' Morena looked over her shoulder to make sure they were alone and leaned forward, lowering her voice to a more intimate level. 'If you're avoiding the question, it means that you're not willing to lie to me and tell me everything's been fine. Which is nice because I don't like being lied to. That then leads me down a path where I realise I've come to mean something to you simply from the fact that you don't want to lie to me. But if I take that path, it opens up a lot of other paths and before I know it I'm lost in a maze, unsure how to get out and wondering if I really want to.'

Nathan's smile increased as she spoke and he nodded. 'You really do have a gift in reading people. That about sums it up. Let me know if you get out of the maze. You can show me the way.'

Morena laughed but any further conversation was cut short as Sally entered the kitchen.

'Now, Morena, you're doing the clinic tomorrow, is that correct?'

'I am rostered on to do the Saturday morning clinic, yes.'

'Good. I won't be able to make it in but you should be fine by yourself. I've pulled all the notes and put them on your desk. It's not too heavy.'

'OK. Thanks, Sal.'

'And, Nathan.' Sally turned to face him. 'Have a good shift at the hospital this weekend. It shouldn't be bad. Nowhere near like schoolies and New Year's Eve, which are the worst times of year here.'

'Australia Day's coming up,' Morena pointed out.

'Is that bad?' Nathan asked.

'Not usually,' Sally responded. 'Although it does depend on what day the 26th falls on. If it's a Friday or a Monday, we have hordes of people down from Adelaide for the long weekend.'

'Thankfully, that's not the case this year,' Morena pointed out. 'There'll be the usual festivities. Markets. Stalls. Everyone flying the flag. Fireworks. Parties.'

'Alcohol shops doing a rip-roaring trade,' Sally continued.

'Thankfully we're not on call at the hospital this year. It was our turn last year,' Morena informed him.

'All righty. I'm out of here,' Sally said. 'Try and have a good weekend.'

When they were left alone, Morena sat back in her chair and sipped her tea, sighing.

'Busy day?' he asked softly.

'Yep. How about you?'

'Same.'

She smiled at him. 'Not bad for a sleepy little medical practice in a retirement destination.'

He nodded. 'Not bad at all. I was thinking, if you're free for dinner tonight we could go over some of the practice paperwork.'

'Oh, be still, my beating heart,' she murmured, and Nathan smiled at her.

'Hey, I've asked you for a proper date and you haven't said another word about it.'

'I was waiting for you to suggest something.'

'I thought you were going to see when you could get a babysitter and then when you didn't mention it, I thought you might have changed your mind.'

'No,' she assured him quickly. 'Haven't changed my mind at all.'

'Well…good. So…when do you want to go on our date?'

Morena smiled. How was it that when he paused like that,

when he raised one eyebrow at a rakish angle as he was doing now, when his brown eyes spoke volumes—*how* was it that he could make her feel so utterly feminine? She felt special when he looked at her like that and no one had made her feel special, not like this.

'Well?' Nathan gave a nervous laugh and shifted in his chair.

'Uh? Oh, sorry. When you look at me like that, I tend to lose the plot a bit.'

His look had been sexy before but it went from sexy to smouldering with desire. He reached over and took her hand in his, caressing it gently with his thumb. 'Don't say things like that, Morena.'

'Why not? It's true.'

'I know. I feel it too but while I want to be with you, to spend time with you, to get to know you much better…when you say things like that I just need to react and not think, but when I don't stop and think, that's when I usually end up making a mess of things.'

She nodded slowly. 'I'm the same. I've spent most of my life doing the right thing, doing what was expected of me, and that's why when you look at me like you are now, when you make my body feel as though it's on fire, when my chest constricts so tightly that I can hardly breathe…Nathan, that's when I don't care about doing the right thing any more and all I can think about right at this moment is that if you don't kiss me, I'm going to faint because I'm so light-headed.'

There was a beat, a moment when the world seemed to stop turning, then Nathan leaned over and captured her mouth with his. Her eyelids fluttered closed and she couldn't believe how right it felt. If she thought she had been breathing heavily before, it was nothing compared to now. It was as though he robbed her of the need to breathe, that it wasn't important. Just as long as he was this close to her, with his lips gently caressing hers, she had no need of air.

There was still so much they didn't know, so much they *should* know, *should* discover, but honestly, as his mouth moved over hers in the most tantalising caress she'd ever experienced, Morena realised his past didn't matter and neither did hers. They'd found each other, they were together, and it was the most electrifying emotion she'd felt in…for ever.

Nothing could compare. Nothing ever would. These moments didn't come around every day and with that blinding flash of clarity he gently opened his mouth to taste the sweetness she offered so generously to him. Her scent, her flavour, everything about her. He was addicted to her and right now he didn't care about anything else. Anyone could walk in, anyone could see them together like this and he wouldn't care just as long as she didn't pull away, didn't deny him the overpowering sense of true life he was experiencing for the first time in over a decade. Simply by pressing his lips to hers, doing what he'd been kept awake thinking of for the past week. But giving in to the urge to do what he wanted, as well as accepting everything she had to give, through it all Nathan was able to pull out the one emotion he never thought he'd ever experience again.

The feeling that after a decade of wandering in the wilderness, he'd finally come home.

CHAPTER EIGHT

MORENA was actually looking forward to going to the hospital on Saturday night. Usually, she suffered through her A and E shift and although she didn't mind helping or taking charge in the variety of cases which came through the hospital's doors at a weekend, it was more time she was away from Connor. As she walked into the A and E department, she was almost tingling with excitement. Excitement because she'd be spending time with Nathan.

After their kiss yesterday, he'd decided against having dinner with her and helping her with the books, telling her he doubted they'd get much work done. Morena had blushed at his words but had understood his meaning. She was positive that they would have been able to control themselves, even after she'd put Connor to bed, but then again, although she'd been desperate for him to kiss her, she wasn't ready for anything else to happen. She doubted he was ready either and so they'd mutually decided—without specifically saying the words out loud—that they would postpone a night of poring over the practice books together.

Even so, she'd all but danced home and had fallen asleep with a dreamy look on her face. She knew that because she'd woken up with the same look on Saturday morning. Nathan had kissed her—and it had been everything she'd fantasised about and so much more.

She'd floated through the Saturday morning clinic before going to her parents' place to have lunch with them and spend an hour with Connor.

'Well, don't you look like the cat who caught the canary?' her mother said as Edward cleared the table, leaving the two women alone.

'What do you mean?'

'You're…glowing, Morena.'

Morena couldn't help the grin that spread across her face. She shrugged and laughed but didn't venture any information.

'Something's happened between you and Nathan. I can tell.' Joyce nodded with satisfaction. 'Does this mean he's going to stay in Victor?'

'Mum! It's nothing like that.'

'Well, if you don't tell me, I'll just keep making assumptions.'

'It's no big deal.'

'Apparently it is.'

'He kissed me. All right? There. Nothing more than that.'

Joyce froze. 'He *kissed* you.'

'Yes.'

'Where?'

Morena frowned. 'On the lips.'

'No, silly child. Where were you?'

'Oh…uh…' Morena looked down at her hands. 'In the kitchen.'

'At your house?' Her mother's eyebrows hit her hairline.

'No…um…at the practice.'

'Morena! Anyone could have walked in. If you're going to start an affair with a man, then, please, a bit of discretion.'

'Start an affair? Discretion? Mum. It was just a kiss!'

'Not to see you looking all dreamy-eyed it wasn't. Not

just a kiss at any rate.' Joyce crossed her arms, clearly displeased.

'Why are you upset? I thought you liked Nathan.'

'I do. It's got nothing to do with that, Morena. It's this town. You've been gossiped about enough for my liking, and I don't want to see you put through the wringer one more time just for laughs. Whatever it is that is going on between you and Nathan—keep a lid on it, at least until you're sure because if you're not and he does leave at the end of his contract, it'll be you who is left with the sidelong glances and whispered conversation that seem to stop abruptly when you come into view.'

Morena listened carefully, comprehending her mother's point and sorting through it in her own mind.

'How do you feel about him?' Joyce continued. 'Are you in love with him?'

'Mum.' Morena shook her head. 'I still don't know him that well.'

'Then be careful, darling. You know your father and I are there for you, whatever happens but don't rush into things.'

'Rush into things? You and Dad were practically matchmaking us during these past weeks.'

'It wasn't meant to be like that. Of course we want your happiness and your father certainly thinks very highly of Nathan. If Nathan is the man for you, that's just wonderful. If he's not and you lose your heart to him, then we'll be there to help you recover, just as we were after Bruce. It's what parents do—they support their children.'

'Thanks.'

'But they also expect their children to have a modicum of sense.'

'I do.'

'I know but…' Joyce stopped and bit her lip.

'But I didn't have sense where Bruce was concerned. It's

all right, Mum. You can say it. You can be honest with me.'
Morena sighed and stood to pace the room, glancing down at
Connor, who was lying on the floor playing with his hanging-
toy frame. 'I know I went through a lot when Bruce left and,
yes, maybe I was infatuated, but I've grown up, Mum. I've
changed. I know myself better now than I did two years ago.
It's surviving the battle that makes us stronger, and I certainly wouldn't be where I am without you and Dad.' She
smiled at her son. 'And Connor, of course.'

She paused for a moment then went on. 'I haven't forgotten what it was like when Bruce left. I haven't forgotten that
desolation or the anguish. I doubt I ever will. I know that if
Nathan decides to leave Victor Harbor I will no doubt have
my heart break a little more than before. But if I turn away
from these feelings I have for him, if I deny them and lock
myself up, then I'm letting Bruce win. He destroyed my self-
confidence in so many ways and being able to trust again is
one of them. I don't know what's going to happen with
Nathan, Mum. All I know is that when he looks at me, when
he touches me, when he holds my hand and tucks a stray
strand of hair back behind my ear, I feel…I feel like a woman,
a *desirable* woman. And it's been far too long since I felt that
way. I've been so busy concentrating on pulling myself
together, with the practice, with Connor, that I feel as though
I've forgotten what it feels like to be a woman. Nathan makes
me remember. It's as though he's brought me back to life and
even if nothing else comes from our time together, I have *that*
to thank him for.'

Morena stood in front of her mother, waiting for her
response, her counsel, her blessing.

'You certainly have thought this through,' Joyce finally
said. 'And I'm proud of you for doing so.'

'Thanks.'

'It's time for you to go to the hospital.'

Morena glanced up at the clock and gave a strangled gasp. 'Is that the time?'

'It is.' Joyce stood and walked over to her daughter, hugging her close. 'I'm proud of you, darling, but know that your father and I are here for you.'

'Thanks,' Morena said again.

'Ready to go?' Edward said from the doorway.

'I am. Are you coming with me?' she asked as she bent down to smother Connor with kisses.

'There are a few patients I want to check on.'

'All right.'

'I'll come by later and pick him up,' Joyce said. 'Connor will enjoy the ride and hopefully he'll fall asleep in the back of the car on the way home.'

After saying goodbye to her mother and her son, Morena drove Edward to the hospital.

'Had a nice chat with your mum?' he asked.

'Yes. How much of it did you hear?' She wasn't fooled a bit into thinking her father hadn't been listening.

'Most of it and I, too, am proud of you, princess.'

'Thanks, Dad.'

'Bruce may have made you grow up a bit faster than you probably would have liked, but those hardships and challenges you've faced have made you stronger. Your mother was right, though. Take things slow with Nathan. He's a good man, Morena, nothing like Bruce, but he's still a man with his own sorting out to do.'

'I know.'

Edward was surprised at that. 'He's confided in you?'

'Some. Why? Has he said anything to you?'

'No. Not that I expected him to. Well, well, well…Perhaps there's even more to Nathan Young than meets the eye.'

'Meaning?'

'Meaning maybe he's ready to move on as well.'

'Hmm.' Morena pulled into the hospital car park and heard her father exclaim in excited delight at the motorbike she'd parked next to. While he walked around the machine, she didn't give it a second thought, her anxiety at seeing Nathan again starting to rise. Would things still be light and jovial between them? She didn't know.

All she did know was that Nathan made her feel like she could take on the world. Before she'd met him, the weight on her shoulders had been enormous, what with her father's failing health, her taking over the practice on her own, sorting out all the legal issues with Bruce and, of course, being the sole parent to the most gorgeous little boy in the world.

Then almost with a snap of his fingers, he'd helped restore her self-confidence because he found her both intelligent and desirable. He'd made her realise that second chances like that didn't fall into your lap every day and she'd be insane not to take the frightening step forward into the unknown. He'd made her realise that she still had a life in front of her, a life she was more than willing to share with him. The fact that it was crazy to be thinking this way, to be feeling this way, didn't bother her at all any more. She was going to go for it with Nathan and see what happened. If she ended up with egg on her face, well, she'd have to wipe it off. She'd survived Bruce and everything he'd done to her to bring her down, she'd survived the gossip that had spread like wildfire around the town, and, more importantly, she had triumphed. If it happened that things *didn't* turn out right with Nathan, then she would survive that, too…but she desperately didn't want things to go wrong.

The instant she saw him, her smile brightened, her eyes twinkled with delight and there was a lightness to her stride.

'Hi, there.' He was sitting at the nurses' station, writing up a set of notes. Several of the staff were hanging around as well.

'Hi.' He briefly looked up but continued with his work.

'So…been busy?' She asked the question as a general one but willed Nathan to answer.

'Steady,' he reported.

'Oh, Nathan, you're being modest,' Zoe, one of the nurses, gushed. 'We had a man come in with massive pain down his left arm and decreased breathing, and where we all thought it was a heart attack, Nathan quickly realised it was anxiety instead. It was amazing.'

Morena nodded at the nurse, who wasn't one of their regulars but had been sent from an agency to cover a member of staff who was off sick. 'Was it, now?' She raised her eyebrows with interest and glanced at Nathan. 'Gee, I'm sorry I missed it.'

'Oh, he was so great. So charming, settling the old man and his wife. They were so grateful but, then…' Zoe paused and fluttered her eyelashes at Nathan, sighing with dramatic effect. 'He's a doctor and he's used to saving people's lives. At least, that's what he told them.' Zoe placed a light hand on Nathan's arm. 'You were *so* great.'

'Thanks,' was all he said, and snapped the file he'd been writing in shut. He stood, and both women stepped back. 'Now that you're here, Morena, I'll go have a quick cup of coffee.'

'Sure.' As their gazes met, she could see that he wasn't in the best of moods. Back was the man she'd met on his first day, his mask in place…but he was still just as sexy. Was it the cases? Was it the gushing nurse? Was it her? Why was he looking reserved once more?

Although she wanted nothing more than to go with him and sit and chat, she managed to get Zoe to focus long enough to give her an update on the patients who were currently being treated in the accident and emergency department.

Her father had come in, made his presence known to the nurses in A and E and then headed off to the wards to catch up with his old friends under the pretence of checking on them in a medical capacity.

Fifteen minutes later, there was still no sign of Nathan and although the amount of time he was taking to have his break wasn't an issue, Morena was starting to get concerned about him. She was about to go and look for him when the phone on the desk rang and she automatically picked it up.

'A and E, Dr Camden.'

'Morena, it's Summer.'

'What's happened?' Morena instantly reached for a pen to receive the report the paramedic was about to deliver.

'Teenage boy left the walking track on Granite Island and fell down a cliff. He was larking about with his friends and lost his balance.'

Morena sighed. 'Is it the section above where the tram comes in?'

'Yes. It needs to be better fenced but we'll leave that for now. Injuries include possible fractures to both feet, right tibia and fibula, lacerations, bruising and mild concussion.'

'He's conscious?'

'Yes, but lost consciousness just after the accident happened, according to his mates.'

'How old is he?'

'Seventeen.'

'Ah, the invincible age.'

'We've stabilised him and administered analgesia. We're about two minutes away.'

'Right. We'll be ready.' Morena rang off and sent Zoe in search of Nathan while she went into the emergency room set up for situations such as this and started to get a few things ready. She also placed a call to Radiology to let them know she'd be bringing a patient down. 'He'll probably require foot, leg and spinal X-rays, as well as a CT scan of his head,' she told them.

'Righto,' Alan, the radiographer said.

'You need me?' Nathan appeared in the doorway just as Morena was hanging up the phone. She turned to face him, wondering if he really wanted her to answer that question. The answer, of course, was a resounding 'yes', but she was positive she was interpreting it in a completely different way from the one he'd intended.

'Patient coming in suffering from multiple trauma.' She gave him the information Summer had rung through.

'Do you transfer patients like that?'

'It depends. If the breaks are straightforward and we can deal with them, then there's no reason. However, on this occasion, given the extent of the injuries, it may actually be better. Flinders Medical Centre is one hour's drive via ambulance for those non-urgent cases or a short fifteen-minute helicopter ride. We'll check him out first.'

Nathan nodded but didn't say anything more. Morena hesitated for a moment and then stepped closer so her words didn't carry. 'Nathan…is anything wrong?'

He looked down at her, first at her lips then back to meet her eyes. Taking a breath, he went to speak but they were interrupted by Zoe coming into the room.

'I can hear ambulance sirens,' she said in an excited singsongy voice, as though she was enjoying herself. 'Morena—just wait until you see Nathan in action. He's *so* amazing.'

Nathan, who had his back to Zoe, rubbed his hand over his face and closed his eyes for a second.

'Zoe, go and greet the ambulance, please,' Morena instructed, and the bubbly nurse headed out. Morena smiled apologetically up at Nathan. 'Take a deep breath. She's rostered on all weekend.'

'Right.' He nodded but didn't return her smile, didn't make any effort to say or do anything else, and Morena was both concerned and a little hurt. Perhaps it wasn't Zoe who was annoying him. Perhaps it really was her? Insecurities began to raise their ugly heads again but there was no time for them right now and she willingly pushed them aside in order to concentrate on her job.

Morena turned from him and went to the sink to wash her hands and pull on a pair of gloves, before pulling out a disposable gown. Without a word Nathan followed suit and within a moment Summer and her colleague were wheeling their patient in on the stretcher. Morena reached for the pat slide and on the count of three they transferred the patient to the hospital barouche while Summer ran through the list of injuries once more.

Nathan was checking the patient's pupils while Morena took a stethoscope from the drawer and listened to her patient's heartbeat.

'Hey, there,' Morena said to the boy, who looked to be about thirteen rather than seventeen.

'Hi,' he replied weakly.

'Pupils equal and reacting to light,' Nathan reported.

Morena nodded and took the stethoscope from her ears, slinging it around her neck. 'I'm Morena. What's your name?'

'Are you a doctor here?'

'I am. This is Nathan. What's your name?'

'Adam.'

'Can you remember what happened, Adam?' Morena smiled her thanks at Summer as the ambulance officers left them to it. Nathan was already assessing Adam's injuries and taking general observations while he spoke.

'I was just mucking around with my mates and I lost my footing and slipped. It was all so sudden and I didn't know the rocks were that loose and…' Tears started to gather in his eyes and Morena placed a gentle hand on his arm.

'It's all right. Are you a local or have you come down from Adelaide for the day?'

'Adelaide.'

'Right. We'll need to contact your parents and—'

'My mates have already called them.'

'Good. By the time your parents arrive, we'll have you settled.' Morena inspected the lump on Adam's head. There was quite a large amount of blood but as she gently cleaned the area so she could take a closer look, she found the laceration wasn't too deep. 'You'll need a few stitches here,' she said, 'but on the whole, it's not too bad.'

'Do you really remember falling or are you just going on what your mates told you?' Nathan asked, coming to stand beside Morena so his patient could see who he was talking to.

'I remember being on the track, you know, walking around, and I remember being up the top and yelling and then…I was in pain and people were leaning over me.'

Nathan nodded and took the boy's blood pressure. It was slightly elevated, which was common in this sort of situation. 'You've been very lucky, Adam. You've hurt both of your feet quite badly and have quite a few broken bones, but we'll get you off to X-Ray so we can assess the full extent of the damage.'

'Are you in any pain?' Morena asked.

'No. The ambulance lady gave me something, I don't know what, but it's OK.'

'All right, then, we'll get you off to X-Ray.'

'I've written up the request form,' Nathan told her, and handed it across to Zoe who'd been willingly assisting him in his examination of the patient. 'I've requested radiographs of both feet, antero-posterior views of the right tibia, spinal column and skull. Did you want a CT of the head?' he asked Morena, and she nodded.

'We can get that organised afterwards.' She turned her attention to Adam. 'Have you vomited at all? Been feeling sick?'

'No. Is that a good thing?'

'Yes.' She smiled at him. 'You'll be fine—in time.'

'Are you sure?' There it was again, that total vulnerability, and despite how much boys his age often thought of themselves as adults, when situations like this occurred, they often realised they needed their mothers just as much as a seven-year-old did.

'I'm sure. Zoe will take you to X-Ray now. The sooner we know what you've done, the sooner we'll know exactly how to fix it.'

After he'd been wheeled out, Nathan gave her a look. 'Well, he's smitten with you.'

'I doubt it. I'm just a mother figure.'

'You're very good at it,' Nathan responded, before pulling off his gloves and walking from the room. Morena frowned, not at all sure what to make of his comments, but as she had notes to write up, she let it go. When she returned to the nurses' station, Nathan wasn't anywhere around and only reappeared from who knew where when Adam returned with his X-rays.

Morena hooked them up on the viewer. 'Three fractured metatarsals on the left and two on the right, as well as a fracture to the left calcaneous. This kid isn't going to be able to walk for a while.' She sighed. 'Right tib and fib.' She shook her head. 'The fracture's impacted.'

'That'll need wiring,' Nathan agreed, standing behind her. He was quite close, so close that she could feel the heat radiating from his body. The scent she equated with him wound itself around her like a warm welcome and she swallowed over the growing sense of anticipation she'd managed to control since first seeing him earlier.

'Right. Surgery it is.'

'Do you have an orthopaedic surgeon here in Victor Harbor?'

'We have surgeons who come and do clinics and elective lists but not one for this sort of thing. No, we'll get Adam transferred to Flinders Medical Centre, that's the closest major hospital to here.'

'Thankfully, the skull looks intact, as well as the spine,' Nathan remarked, leaning forward to point to the radiograph in question. As he did, his arm brushed Morena's and she gasped at the contact. 'Sorry.' The word was barely audible and he shifted so they weren't touching any more.

'He's a lucky lad,' Nathan added, swallowing over the effect Morena had on him. He'd been doing his best to control the desire that had flooded through him the instant he'd laid eyes on her that afternoon. He *had* to control himself, especially after the kiss they'd shared yesterday. He'd had a terrible night—the worst since meeting her—as he'd stayed awake, feeling guilty over kissing a woman who wasn't his wife.

'You're not wrong,' Morena said, and he noticed the shakiness to her words. 'My guess is bruising around the coccyx if anything, but according to these scans, he's doing well.' She turned to look for the CT films and when she couldn't find any, she looked around for Zoe. The nurse was just coming out of one of the treatment rooms, heading in their direction. 'Zoe, has Adam had the CT scan yet?'

'The machine's not working properly,' Zoe reported, and Morena rolled her eyes. 'They've been having problems with it all week long.'

She sighed. 'Right. As he hasn't vomited and his pupils were reacting normally to light…' She looked at Nathan for confirmation on this and he nodded. 'And the skull and spinal X-rays show no damage so it should be safe for him to be transferred to Adelaide without the CT. They can do it there.'

'Agreed,' Nathan said. 'Zoe, can you go and do his obs again, please?'

'Sure thing, cutie.' She winked at him as she headed off, swishing her hips.

'Yikes. She's getting more obvious.'

'Tell me about it.' Nathan slumped into one of the chairs. 'Are all the nurses here like her?'

Morena shook her head and smiled. 'You were able to handle the staff at the nursing home, not to mention Mrs Matthews flirting with you. Then there were the ladies at the retirement village who were so blatantly obvious in their attentions that I thought their ovaries might start working again. Oh, and also Mrs Henderson, who you managed to charm on your very first day at work. Mrs Henderson,' she said with emphasis, 'who never smiles or has a kind word for anyone, and there you were, charming her so much she was rushing home to bake biscuits for you—and you're worried about Zoe?' she finished incredulously.

Nathan frowned. 'When you put it that way…'

'Trust me. You can handle her.'

'But can I handle you?' The words were said with a resigned sigh and Morena could only stare at him.

'What does that mean?' Concern was etched all over her face and Nathan shook his head and stood.

'I don't know.' He raked a hand through his hair, making it stick out slightly. Morena couldn't help but smile at how gorgeous he looked…gorgeous and vulnerable. 'I can't think straight, I…I hardly slept last night. I feel…horrible and guilty because I want to be with you, but at the same time I know it's wrong.'

'Why is it wrong?' Morena glanced around them, knowing this wasn't the time or the place. 'Look, we're off in a few more hours so how about coming back to my apartment for dinner? Nothing flash—although I do have a bottle of Shiraz from one of the local wineries.' Nathan smiled at her words. 'And we just talk. Sort some things out. What do you think?'

Nathan looked around him, noticing that Zoe was headed back in their direction. 'OK.'

'Good.' Morena wanted to touch him, hug him, to reassure him that it was all right for him to be stepping out of his comfort zone, but she knew it wouldn't be the right thing to do and the last thing she needed right now was to have him withdraw from her. Whatever it was between them was far too important to risk on a wrong move. They continued to work through their shift, with both of them talking to Adam's parents when they arrived and staying on until their patient had been successfully airlifted off to FMC.

Twenty minutes later they received another call and this time Nathan took down the details. After he'd put down the phone, he looked at Morena. 'That was Summer. MVA ten minutes out of town. She's on her way here to collect us as she said they'll definitely need us out on site for retrieval.'

'OK.' Morena turned to Zoe, who'd walked over as Nathan had spoken. 'Zoe, find my father and let him know what's happened. He can cover A and E until we get back. Next, ring Flinders, let them know we have an MVA and to send the helicopter for transfer. I'll need three more nurses called in as well. Any questions, you ask my father.'

'Got it,' Zoe said, and for a moment Morena thought things might be looking up before Zoe said, 'Who's your father?'

Rolling her eyes, Morena wrote everything down for her while Nathan was busy going through cupboards, trying to find the things he thought they might need. 'We need to change,' Morena told him, and led him to the changing rooms where they both changed into orange retrieval overalls. When the ambulance pulled up, they were both ready to go. Morena climbed in first and Nathan got in and closed the door, helping her with her seat belt when she couldn't find the clasp.

'Badger's gone ahead in the other ambulance,' Summer said of her colleague.

'Is it just one car? Two?' Morena asked.

'At least three, from what I was told. There's a truck involved, too. Apparently, that came off the road and tipped over. There's one car which has rolled and another blocking traffic heading towards Adelaide.'

'Police?'

'Should beat us there,' Summer said as she concentrated on her driving, the wail of the siren surrounding them as she sped competently through the streets. The sun would be down within an hour and if they could get a handle on the situation before then, it would make all the difference.

When they neared the site, Summer slowed the ambulance and Morena was pleased to see Senior Sergeant Tracey already in attendance and dealing with all the gawkers in the cars on their way back to Adelaide. Summer manoeuvred the ambulance through to get as close to the crash site as possible and as they passed the first car, Morena gasped. The car had obviously rolled several times and although it was now upright, the roof was compressed.

She gasped. 'How is anyone meant to survive that?'

'People have survived worse,' was all he said, and she knew he was right. This wasn't the first MVA she'd attended, neither would it be the last. Two other cars were strewn over the road, one blocking Adelaide traffic, as had been reported. Thankfully, the driver of that car seemed to be not too bad as he was standing beside the car, talking to one of the police officers, pointing and talking earnestly. He did, however, have blood trickling down his forehead so he'd need to be checked for head injury.

The other car was off on the gravel shoulder, battered and beaten from all sides but not as bad as the one that had rolled. The truck was right off the road and on its side on the dry grassed area, its load scattered around.

'Thank goodness it wasn't a fuel tanker,' Summer said as she finally brought the ambulance to a stop. They all bundled out, taking their medical kits with them.

'Morena—you take the roll-over,' Nathan said with authority. 'I'll check out this car here...' he pointed to the car on the shoulder '...and then the truck driver. Summer, deal with the driver who's talking to the police officer. Where's your colleague?'

'Badger?' She looked around. 'Over there with the truck driver.'

Nathan nodded and headed off, glancing back only once to see Morena making her way towards the rolled car. He hoped the occupants weren't in as bad a condition as the car. When he crossed to the car on the shoulder, he shook his head. Even from where he stood he could see the driver—who was the only occupant of the car—slumped forward over the steering wheel at an extremely odd angle. It was impossible to get in through the driver's door so he tried the others, but they were all jammed fast from the impact. The window of the passenger door on the driver's side had been smashed and after he'd carefully knocked away the rest of the glass with the end of his torch, Nathan was able to jimmy the door from the side so it opened. He called out to the driver but received no response. Working his way into the car, he angled his way into the front. He pulled on a pair of gloves and pressed his fingers to the driver's neck. No pulse. Taking out his medical torch, he carefully lifted the man's head and checked his pupils.

'Fixed and dilated,' he said, then checked the time on his watch so he could report the death. Shifting carefully back out of the car, he turned to find himself face to face with a police officer.

'He's dead.' Nathan ripped off his gloves and picked up his medical kit. 'Broken neck. Probably died on impact.'

'Right. I'll get a tarp to cover the car.' The officer hesitated a moment. 'Who are you?'

'Dr Nathan Young,' he said as he headed towards the truck driver, not giving the officer another thought. 'Badger?' Nathan called, and the paramedic came into view. 'Report?'

Badger started to give Nathan a rundown on the truck driver when there was a loud call from the direction of the rolled car.

'Nathan!'

'That's Morena.' Nathan was already heading in her direction. 'You can cope here, can't you, mate?'

'Sure. Go.'

Nathan hurried quickly but carefully to Morena's side. 'What's wrong?'

'I can't get them out. I can't get them out,' she said urgently. Nathan was a little surprised to see her so shaken up.

'Morena?' He put his kit down and placed his hands on her shoulders.

'We're going to need the jaws of life to cut them out. Quick. We need to get that radioed through. It'll have to come from Adelaide. Get it organised now.'

'Hey. Wait a second.' He forced her to look at him but she was still babbling.

'No. This can't be happening. I've *got* to get them out.' She wrenched from his grasp and returned to the car, trying to figure out a way in, trying the handle, but it didn't work.

'Get *who* out? Do you know them?' He was at her side, peering inside the car. He could see a woman in the passenger seat, a man in the driver's seat and… He gulped, feeling instantly ill. A baby in the back.

'Is that a baby?'

'Yes. That's Ivan. That's Kaylee, Mr Dinsmore's daughter. That's her husband Simon. Nathan.' She gripped his hands. 'We *must* get to them. We need to figure it out.'

He nodded, trying to come to terms with the fact that a young baby was in the back. Not just any baby but Mr Dinsmore's youngest grandchild—a baby the same age as Connor. Morena was right. They needed to help this family, especially as this weekend was the anniversary of Mrs Dinsmore's death.

'What's the protocol, Morena?' he asked.

'I can help you there,' a voice said, and Nathan turned. 'Senior Sergeant Tracey,' the man said. 'Who's in the car, Morena?'

'Kaylee Dinsmore.' It didn't matter that Kaylee's surname had changed when she'd married Simon—Tracey knew immediately who she was talking about and Nathan saw his manner change. Everything was different now. The people in this car weren't just unfortunate patients, they were *family*, and if there was one thing he'd learned about small towns, they looked after their own.

'Right.' Tracey nodded and pressed the button on his shoulder radio. 'Where's that fire truck?' he barked. He continued to give orders and receive information while Nathan and Morena continued to try for a way in. Tracey had ordered his young constable to bring over a crowbar and Morena suggested they try to jimmy the boot open in the hope that they could get in that way, but it was impossible. She heard a noise from the car as Nathan and Tracey were wondering if they could get in through the shattered windscreen.

Morena walked to the window and looked inside. It was the baby she could hear crying and she sent up a thankful prayer. The cries were like music to her ears and it gave her hope.

'We won't move them until the roof's been peeled way but we need to get to them to treat them,' Nathan said.

Morena was filled with renewed energy and with the crowbar in her hand, she tried to open Kaylee's passenger door once more, this time managing to prise the metal apart.

'Nathan!' she called, and he came quickly to her side, immediately taking the crowbar and heaving with all his might. Slowly the door began to open and at the same time Kaylee start to rouse. They pushed and pulled, working together, and before they knew it, they were able to get right in to check Kaylee out.

Morena bent down and took her friend's hand. 'Kaylee? Can you hear me? It's Morena.'

'Morena?' Kaylee's voice was soft and dazed. 'Where am I?'

'You've been in an accident. Just stay still. We're going to get you out.'

'Simon? Ivan?' Those were Kaylee's next words and Morena reassured her as best she could. There was still no sign of movement from Simon but from her position she could at least see that he was still breathing.

'I'm going to try Simon's door again,' Nathan said. It only took one small triumph for the adrenaline to surge once more.

Morena was able to keep Kaylee talking while she checked her out, pleased to see that all her friend appeared to be suffering from was cuts and bruises. 'Can you wiggle your toes for me?' she asked, and was rewarded with a very good wiggle. Morena continued to give Kaylee a few tests but was certain her friend's spine wasn't damaged. Still, she fitted a cervical collar around Kaylee's neck just as Nathan made some progress with Simon's door.

'That's what I like to see,' she said, feeling the initial weight of her heart lift dramatically. Ivan was still crying in the back but after hearing his mother's voice, he'd quietened a little. Morena was still trying to figure out how to get to him but at the moment it appeared they could only do that once they'd moved Kaylee or Simon out of the way.

Nathan had managed to prise open Simon's door enough to be able to squeeze into the gap and check the man's injuries. 'Simon?' he called, and after the third time, when Kaylee joined in, Simon finally responded. Everyone breathed a sigh of relief.

The next time Morena took notice of her surroundings, the sun had gone down, bright rescue lights were shining on the accident site and a fire truck was in attendance. She'd been aware that all of these things were happening but only peripherally, her focus having been on her friends.

Badger had managed to help the truck driver out of his vehicle and then driven him to hospital while Summer was just returning from the hospital, having taken the driver of the other car. She came over to see if she could be of any assistance.

'We're just waiting for the jaws of life,' Morena said, feeling the warm evening breeze pick up. She looked up at the gathering clouds and groaned. 'Don't tell me we're going to get a thunderstorm. That's the last thing we need.'

'No rain has been forecast,' Summer said. 'That doesn't mean to say we won't get any lightning.'

Morena rubbed a hand across her eyes, concerned for her friends and especially little Ivan. He was still breathing and was crying every now and then but they weren't able to get to him at all to check him out—not without moving either Kaylee or Simon out of the way. Simon's injuries were more severe than Kaylee's and Morena had already prepared her friend that Simon would need to be airlifted to Flinders Medical Centre for treatment.

'Why today?' Kaylee said again, a fresh bout of tears accompanying her words. 'Why now?'

'I know,' Morena said, and held her friend's hand, offering a tissue. 'But you're all alive. That's a blessing.'

'Dad's not going to cope.'

'Oh, I think you'll find he will. He's as strong as a Mallee bull.'

'But this weekend was supposed to be…' She trailed off as Ivan began to cry again.

'Shh,' Morena soothed, not sure whether she was talking to baby or mother or both. 'We're getting you out. We're looking after you. We're not going to let anything happen to you, are we, Nathan?'

'Most certainly not,' he replied firmly.

Kaylee sniffed then gave Morena a little smile. 'I can see why you like him.'

Morena glanced at Nathan, who met and held her gaze for a moment.

'Keep this one,' Kaylee continued, obviously not caring about any sort of embarrassment either party might feel.

'Thanks for the advice,' was all Morena said, but she found it difficult to look away. Nathan was smiling at her. It wasn't one of his bright, beaming smiles, which was guaranteed to make her knees go weak. No, this was a small, unsure smile, which was filled with hope. It didn't make her knees go weak because it went straight to her heart, filling it with strength…strength to continue forward. Hope and strength. Good combinations.

There was a loud crack from above and everyone looked up. The sky lit up for a second or two. Nathan straightened from where he'd just finished performing Simon's observations and looked over to the truck, which was on its side. Work crews were busy clearing up as much debris as they could. Another crack, the air around them filled with electricity and Nathan felt the hairs on the back of his neck stand on end. The lightning, the dry brown grass, a damaged truck—it was a bad combination, and no sooner had the thoughts passed through his head than he heard shouts from the crews working around the truck.

'Fire. It's on fire!' One yelled.

'Everyone move!' Tracey bellowed, people not needing the instruction to make sure they were out of the way. Morena watched—everything happening so fast, turning the situation from one of relative control to one of disastrous proportions in a matter of seconds.

She could see flames starting to lick at the grass, their height and colour being assisted by the warm wind, picking it up and spreading it quickly. The fire crews were rushing around, getting into position to fight it. Everything seemed to be happening in slow motion. She looked over at Nathan, he turned to look at her and with unspoken communication they made the decisions that needed to be made. The danger of the fire was imminent and evacuation was a must. There was no more time to wait.

'Summer,' Morena said, bending down. 'We need to get Kaylee and Simon out.' Summer was quick to hand Morena the heavy-duty scissors to cut Kaylee from her seat belt. 'I can manage her. Help Nathan.'

Summer did as she was told and Morena managed to get Kaylee out, glad she'd completely checked her friend earlier for spinal injuries. 'I'll take her,' Tracey said, appearing by Morena's side the instant Kaylee was out.

'Ivan. What about Ivan?' Kaylee was sobbing.

'We'll get him. We'll get him out,' Morena said, and quickly bent into the car, trying to work her way through to the back of the car. She could squeeze through to a certain point but her arms weren't long enough to reach Ivan. She did manage to get her first good look at him and apart from an egg-shaped bump on his head, he appeared unhurt. The baby capsule he was in had protected him completely, as it was designed to do. They needed to cut him from the harness holding him in so they could get him out, but she couldn't do it. She just couldn't reach him.

'How is he?' Nathan asked as they prepared to move Simon, the stretcher ready and waiting.

'He looks fine but I can't reach him.'

'Help me here for a moment,' Nathan said, and they concentrated on getting Simon out, the heat from the blaze making itself felt. Although the fire crews were battling it, with the wind whipping things up there was no telling whether or not they'd be able to get control.

Morena looked from the fire to Nathan. 'We need to get Ivan out.'

Nathan could hear the hysteria rising in her voice. 'We will.' He took her hands in his. 'I promise you, Morena. Go over to Kaylee. I'll get Ivan out.'

'I'm not leaving you,' she stated firmly.

'It's not safe.'

'I'm not leaving you,' she argued.

'I can get him out,' Nathan said, climbing into the car from the passenger side. He looked in at the small baby, now crying loudly, fear in its voice. Nathan didn't blame him, didn't blame him one bit. Nathan clenched his jaw firmly, determined to save this family. To ensure that Kaylee, Simon and little baby Ivan had many more days ahead of them to spend with Mr Dinsmore. He hadn't been able to save his own wife and unborn child. He hadn't been there—no one had. Well, that wasn't going to happen this time. He was going to save baby Ivan and although the heat from the blaze was increasing every moment, he continued. Reaching forward, he managed to place his hands onto the harness holding Ivan in place. The buckle was stuck.

'Morena. Scissors,' he commanded. He could hear Tracey telling them to evacuate, that he wasn't going to lose two good doctors. Morena ignored him and handed Nathan the implement. Nathan focused, the sweat sliding off him as the heat intensified. With steady and firm hands, he cut the belts, releasing Ivan instantly. The baby began to squirm even more, not being bound so tightly, and for a second Nathan found it difficult to get a grip on him.

'Stay still,' he commanded, and either the shock of a deep voice or the way Nathan had said the words was enough to jolt Ivan long enough for Nathan to slide his large hands beneath the baby and lift him out. As he backed out, he heard Morena calling out to him, her tone laced with fear and trepidation. He glanced out the window and saw an orange fireball heading his way and somehow—he still wasn't sure how—he put on extra speed, adrenaline surging as he used his body to shield the baby and move them both to safety.

Five seconds later the car he'd just pulled Ivan from was engulfed in flames, the heat searing them all, but it was too late. The fire hadn't claimed their lives. They had won!

Nathan collapsed to the ground where Tracey had set up a safety zone, allowing Ivan to be taken from him by Summer. Exhaustion overtook him as he rolled onto his back, breathing heavily.

'Nathan?' Morena was at his side, pressing her fingers to his neck, checking his pulse, placing her hand over his heart.

'Morena.' He opened his eyes and looked up into her worried face. She was incredible. She was lovely, she was amazing, she was…his. He could see it. After such a moment as they'd just lived through there was no denying the way they felt, and he found a modicum of strength from somewhere and placed his fingers about her neck, urging her head down so he could claim her lips.

The kiss was everything—everything she needed.

Nathan was safe. Nathan had saved Ivan. Nathan was kissing her in front of everyone and she didn't care.

CHAPTER NINE

IT SEEMED like hours before they were back at the hospital and their patients seen to. Morena couldn't help but feel that tonight her relationship with Nathan had seemed to define itself. When she'd told her mother they would take things slowly, it now seemed impossible. Their lives had been put in jeopardy and that had changed everything.

Eventually, everything was done and dusted. Kaylee and Ivan were settled in a ward, with Mr Dinsmore sleeping on a fold-out bed by their side. The poor man had looked like the ghost of Christmas past when he'd arrived at the hospital but after seeing his daughter and holding his grandson in his arms, his colour had returned. The scene had brought tears to Morena's eyes and she'd felt Nathan's hand on her shoulder. When she'd looked up at him, he hadn't tried to hide his emotions and she'd witnessed the raw pain from his past.

There was no need of words as she put her arm around his waist and held him close. Simon had been taken by helicopter to Flinders and they'd received an update to say he was out of surgery and off the critical list, doing very well in the intensive care unit.

'Didn't you say something a few hours ago about dinner?' Nathan murmured, and she smiled up at him.

'Typical male. All you can think about is your empty stomach.'

He looked at her for a moment, then said softly, 'That's not all I'm thinking about.' Morena breathed in his meaning and could see the light in his eyes. 'Let's get changed and get out of here. I'll meet you outside.'

Once she had changed, she headed out, looking around the car park for him. She wondered what sort of car he drove as since his arrival she'd done all the driving. For some reason she'd pictured him in a classic car, but there wasn't a car like that in the car park. Perhaps he'd walked, although it was quite a way from his apartment. Morena frowned then turned when she heard the hospital doors whoosh open. Her mouth whooshed open as well when she saw Nathan carrying a well-worn leather jacket and a motorcycle helmet.

'You ride a motorbike!'

'Problem?'

'You're a doctor!' she said, as though that explained everything.

'I know. Problem?'

'You know the statistics of the types of injuries motorbike riders can face. You would have seen them, treated them, and still you choose to ride one?'

'If it's ridden properly, there's no reason why it isn't any safer than a car. You surprise me, Morena. I didn't have you pegged as a bike-bigot.'

'I am not a bike-bigot. I resent that. I'm just…' She trailed off.

'Just what?' He prompted.

'You know what? None of my business.' She shook her head and headed to her car, which she'd parked next to the bike in question when she'd arrived, not realising it was Nathan's. She rounded on him a second later. 'Have you ever had an accident?'

'Not a serious one. In fact, I had a more serious accident in a car so there goes all your theories.'

'They're not *theories*. There's substantiated and well-documented medical evidence.'

'Why is this such a problem for you?' He paused, trying to figure her out. 'Did Bruce ride a bike?'

Morena scoffed at that. 'No way. Too…ordinary for the likes of him.' She watched him pull on his jacket, liking the way it fitted his body, liking the way it enhanced his dark good looks, liking the way it automatically turned him into a bad boy. Then dawning realisation crossed her face. 'Of course. You ride the bike because it represents a certain level of freedom you feel you require.' Glad she'd finally figured out the puzzle, she unlocked her car and climbed in. 'Right, then. I've got to go pick up Connor and then I'll meet you at my place.'

'Right. Do you want me to pick up some take-away?' He paused. 'Is there anything open at this time of night?'

'It's only just after ten o'clock. Try the Chinese restaurant.'

'Ten o'clock? Why does it feel so much later?'

'Gee. I wonder.' She smiled at him.

'Do I need to get anything specific for Connor?'

'No. I have all his food prepared.'

'OK, then.' He pulled on his helmet, the visor still up as he swung his leg over the machine she recognised as a Harley-Davidson. 'See you at your place.' He winked at her, slid the visor into place and revved the engine to life. Morena couldn't help it—she was excited by the picture he made.

By the time Morena made it home, surprised to have found Connor wide awake and grizzling at her mother's house, Nathan was standing outside her apartment, two plastic bags in his hands.

'Have you been waiting long?' she asked as she unbuckled Connor and took him from the car. The baby was crying loudly.

'No.'

'Sorry. I was longer than I thought. Connor's in an uncooperative mood, if you hadn't guessed. He should have been asleep but Mum said he's been completely unsettled. Probably his teeth.' She half expected Nathan to put his bags down and make a quick excuse before riding off into the night, but he surprised her by taking her keys from her and opening the door.

'We'll get him sorted,' Nathan said, taking the bags through to the kitchen.

Morena put her son on the floor on his play-mat and the baby only screamed louder. 'I just need to get a few things from the car,' she said, dashing outside again. Oh, Connor. If only he'd been co-operative, tonight of all nights. She was totally exhausted and was also worried that Nathan was going to run off at any second, especially with a grumpy baby around, given that he wasn't a big fan of children. She pushed the thought away, not wanting to deal with that one right now.

When she went back inside it was to find that Connor had stopped crying. Astounded, she stood in the doorway and stared. Nathan had picked him up and was cradling him in his arms, talking gently to him.

'There, now. That's better. Don't go giving your mum a hard time, mate. She's doing a terrific job and she loves you so very much, even I can see it. So don't you go belly-aching when you should be smiling at her. Got that?'

'I think he has,' Morena said, and Nathan spun around to look at her.

'Sorry. Didn't hear you.'

'I'm not surprised with the noise Connor was making. It's enough to make your ears ring for days after he's stopped.' She laughed as she closed the door, putting the baby bag and her work bag down by the door. 'Here, I'll take him,' she said, crossing to his side.

'No. He's OK.' Nathan looked down at his charge and Morena couldn't believe the light that was shining in his brown eyes. It seemed that Connor had worked his magic over Nathan as well as everyone else he'd met. 'Why don't you get his dinner ready while he's settled?'

'Good idea.' Not wanting to break the bond she only wished could form, Morena headed into the kitchen, peeking in the bags he'd brought and putting a few things, like the frozen ice-cream dessert he'd bought, into the freezer so it didn't melt. She switched on the air-conditioning, especially as Nathan was still standing there with his leather jacket on, and set about her work.

Connor, surprisingly, remained quiet and quite content in Nathan's arms until she was ready, and once he'd had his very late dinner, he started to settle down.

'Mum said he had a late sleep this afternoon so it's not surprising he was a bit grumpy.' She ran her hand lovingly over Connor's downy head. 'Poor darling.' As she did that, he snuggled closer to her. 'Sorry about our dinner. It'll have to wait until I have him settled.'

'It's fine. It can easily be reheated.'

'OK. Well…I guess I'll change my son, feed my son and then put my son to bed.' She lifted Connor up and kissed his tummy, being rewarded with a tired little giggle.

'Where do you…uh…usually breastfeed him?' Nathan asked.

'Out here, but I can do it in his room tonight if it makes you feel uncomfortable.'

'No. It's fine.'

'I usually just have the television on. I think the background noise helps him to drift off, to tell you the truth.'

'Don't change his routine simply because I'm here.'

Morena smiled at him. 'All right, then.' She set about her son's nighttime routine, still half expecting Nathan to go into the kitchen and busy himself in there while she sat on the lounge and fed Connor, but once more Nathan surprised her by coming and sitting beside her, his arm along the back of the lounge as they watched television in a companionable silence.

When she'd finished and Connor was settled for the night, she came back out to find Nathan had been through her CD collection, had put on some jazz and was preparing their food in the kitchen. 'Whew,' she sighed and accepted the glass of wine he handed her. 'Thanks.' She took a sip then set the glass down on the bench. 'What can I do to help?'

Nathan turned to face her. 'Honestly? You can help by telling me what's going on between us.'

Morena was a little taken aback at his words but she guessed she couldn't blame him. Tonight had been such a mixture of emotions it was difficult to try to make sense out of them herself.

'Why don't we get dinner ready and chat while we eat?'

'Look, just tell me now. How do you feel about me?'

'How…?' Morena shook her head. 'You don't start off with the easy questions, do you?' She picked up the glass of wine he'd handed her and took another sip. 'Well…uh…you make me feel…special. You're on my wavelength, which, I have to add, is a very difficult thing to find…someone on your wavelength, I mean.' She shrugged. 'Look at us, Nathan. We've known each for such a short time and we're having this sort of conversation.'

'But what about Bruce?'

'What about him? What does he have to do with this?'

'He hurt you. You vowed never to get hurt again.'

'Will you hurt me?'

Nathan stopped and looked up at the ceiling for a moment, closing his eyes before meeting her eyes again. 'Never willingly, Morena.'

'So I guess, as you've asked about my ex-husband, I should ask about your wife. Is that what's bothering you?'

'Bothering me?' He laughed without humour. 'Yeah. You could say that. I kissed you yesterday. Then I kissed you tonight. I kissed another woman! For the first time in ten years I kissed someone who wasn't Lila.'

'And I'm guessing you didn't sleep a wink because you were beating yourself up with guilt about it.'

He waited a moment and she wasn't sure whether she'd pushed him too far and too fast, but he had been the one to start this subject for discussion and she sincerely hoped he wasn't going to walk away just as they were getting to the heart of it.

'Did you sleep last night?'

'Yes. Oh, yes.' She sighed with longing and it was enough to make Nathan want to scoop her into his arms but he resisted…for now.

'You weren't bothered by memories of Bruce?'

'No way. I understand this is different for both of us, Nathan. My husband hurt me and left. Your wife died. Those are two completely different scenarios and you can't expect us to have similar reactions.'

'Yet you're able to move on, to take the chance of getting hurt, to trust again?'

She looked into his eyes, wanting him to see how serious she was. 'Yes.'

'You'd trust me?'

'I already do. Nathan, I'm willing for you to help me with the business side of the practice, I'm willing to let you into my home, I'm willing to let you near my son. I'm willing to let you into my life. If someone had told me last month that I would be ready for such a huge change, I would have laughed in their face and said they were ridiculous. But now…meeting you, talking to you, being with you…' She sighed. 'Nathan, it's as though you've brought me to life again. I'm a woman who believes in second chances and although I wasn't sure one existed for me, you've shown me otherwise.'

'So you're saying that this isn't just some short-term romance for you? This isn't just a rebound thing because I find you sexy?'

'No, but the "finding me sexy" part does tend to help.' She smiled at him but he didn't return it. It didn't matter. 'We communicate, Nathan. Bruce and I *never* communicated like this, never talked like this, not even at the start of our relationship.'

'Mr Dinsmore said you don't trust easily.'

'Did he? I guess he knows me better than I thought. Well, he's right.'

'Yet you trust me.'

'I do.'

'With what?'

'With everything. With my practice, my son, my heart…'

There was sadness in Nathan's eyes and she wanted above everything else to remove it, to let him know that there was hope for them. 'This sort of connection we have, Nathan, it doesn't come along every day. It's rare—and yet we found it. Isn't that amazing?'

He nodded slowly.

'Well, you've asked how I feel about you so now I think it's your turn. How do you feel about me?'

'Shaken.' He raked an unsteady hand through his hair. 'I can't stop thinking about that kiss.'

'I know. Neither can I.'

'But I'm also not sure this is the right thing to do.'

'You and me?'

'Yes. You, me, Connor.'

'Tonight…you were holding him.'

'I know and it was…like heaven.' His eyes softened. 'I've been fighting it for too long, not wanting to get involved with anyone. It's why I move and keep on moving. I've always found it difficult to be around pregnant women, seeing young babies, but tonight, seeing Connor there, crying, seeing you being so harried and trying to cope with the responsibility of raising him all on your own…I don't know, Morena, something just clicked. Maybe it had something to do with rescuing Ivan, with helping keep Kaylee's family together. I don't know but I'd picked up Connor even before I knew what I was doing. It was instinct.'

'And?' She prompted when he stopped.

'And I couldn't believe how incredible it felt to hold him in my arms. To feel his soft skin with my fingers, to have him look up at me with those big blue eyes that are so much like his mother's and hear him quieten. He's a gorgeous little boy and your ex-husband was a total moron for even *suggesting* you terminate the pregnancy.'

'No argument there.'

'Connor…' He breathed out and shook his head. 'He's helped to knock down a huge section of the walls I've surrounded myself with over the years.'

'Have I knocked down any walls?' she asked hesitantly.

'Yes. Yes, you have.' Nathan held out his arms and she went willingly into them. 'Enough. For now.'

'Yes.' Morena closed her eyes and rested her head against his chest, listening to his heart beating beneath her ear. 'You're alive,' she told him.

'I am.'

Morena absorbed everything about him, committing it all

to memory so she could keep it with her for ever. She had no idea how this could be, no idea how to cope with incredible emotions she'd never felt before, but right now none of that mattered. Right now, all she was concerned with was being with him, spending time with him. She knew next to nothing about him and surprisingly she didn't care. Her heart knew him, knew him so well it was as though they'd been destined to meet, and as she stood there, his arms holding her firmly to him, Morena realised she'd fallen in love with him. It was ridiculous—*totally* ridiculous—but true, and she hugged him closer.

Nathan responded to that by moving gently from side to side, swaying in time to the music he'd put on, and Morena willingly went with him. Dancing in the kitchen, two glasses of wine on the bench, the aromas of the food he'd heated gently filling the air, enticing the atmosphere to be one of memory making.

'This is relaxing.'

Morena eased back and looked up at him as he spoke, her eyes reflecting she felt exactly the same way. He took her hand in his and continued to dance around the small kitchen, and at the next big crescendo in the music Nathan gently spun her away from him and then back again.

Morena laughed. 'You're a very good dancer.'

'Thank you. You're not too bad yourself.'

'Connor and I dance together all the time.'

'I'll bet you lead.'

'You're right, I do.' She brushed her fingers through his hair. 'It's nice not to have to lead for once.'

Nathan understood her meaning and accepted it. She was a woman who carried so much on her gorgeous shoulders and if he could give her some relief from that, even if it was just for a few hours, he was willing to do so. He could give—and she would accept. It was nice to be able to give to someone else in that way and it was another emotion, a very personal one, he hadn't experienced for far too long.

'Why don't you sit down and I'll finish getting dinner ready? Go put your feet up.'

'That's sweet. Why don't I set the table and help you instead?'

'You don't want to relax?'

'I don't want to be too far from you,' she confessed with a shy smile. 'The lounge is *wa-ay-y* over there. Far too far.'

Nathan was thrilled, excited by her answer, by her need to be near him. 'Fair enough.' He spun her out once more, winking at her before pressing his lips to her hand and reluctantly letting it go.

They managed to get through dinner, the conversation light and general. Neither seemed eager to delve into anything more serious that might break the mood.

Nothing mattered except being together, sharing a meal, a glass of wine, the soothing sounds of jazz filling the air. It was the most pleasant and romantic evening Morena could ever remember having.

'Thank you,' she said as he picked up his motorbike helmet and jacket. It was just after midnight and Nathan had declared it was time for him to leave, although it was the last thing he wanted to do.

'For?'

'Hmm, there are so many things, it's hard to choose which one. I guess…thank you for a fantastic evening. I can't remember ever having a more relaxing and enjoyable time.'

'Ever?'

'Nope.' She shook her head slowly for emphasis.

Nathan put his jacket on and then took her hand in his free one. 'Walk me to my bike.'

'OK. Let me just check on Connor.'

Nathan nodded and watched her go to her son's room. He

moved closer and stood in the doorway, amazed at the way she was affecting him. She stood by her son's cot and ran her hand over his soft head and down his back, patting him gently. She was a dedicated and loving mother and although he knew that, to see it in action was starting to get to him emotionally. He'd never been given the opportunity to hold his son, to cuddle his son, to touch him while he slept—as Morena was doing with Connor. And what was most surprising of all was that usually when Nathan thought about things like that, the first emotion to swamp him was guilt, but this time it was one of resigned sadness.

He'd missed it all. The birth of his son, those first few days when everything was new. The way his son would have felt, the way his heart would have beaten so fast, his scent, his soft, smooth skin untouched by the world. He'd missed it all and all he felt now was a deep sadness.

Turning from the picture before him, Nathan walked to the door, looking over his shoulder as he heard Morena pick up her keys. 'I know I'm not going far, but I'm paranoid,' she said, and he nodded, understanding her need to do absolutely everything in her power to protect her son. They went outside and she locked the apartment door behind her. Nathan held out his hand to her once more and she took it, walking the short distance to the kerb where he'd parked his bike.

'I know you don't have far to go to get back to your place but, please, drive carefully.'

'You mean ride carefully.'

'Whatever. Just be careful.'

'Why?' Nathan let go of her hand as he swung a leg over his bike and put the key into the ignition. He rested his helmet on the fuel tank in front of him and turned to face her.

'Why? Because there are idiots on the roads.'

'Even in sleepy Victor Harbor?'

'Yes.'

'Even at this time of night?'

'Especially at this time of night.'

'I promise to be careful…but why are you so concerned?'

It was then Morena realised he was fishing and she decided to tease him a little. 'Well…because…if anything was to happen to you, I'd be stuck doing all the clinics and house calls.'

'Oh.' His face fell. 'Is that all?'

'I'd also have half the women in town cross with me because they wouldn't be able to flirt with you.'

'Only half?' Nathan raised an eyebrow.

'Oh, the ego!' She smiled.

'What's the real reason?'

'The real reason?'

'Why you want me to be careful?'

'I think you already know.'

He nodded. 'But I need to hear it, Morena.'

She looked into his eyes, the lamp across the street illuminating them enough for her to see that he really did need the words, needed the reassurance that what they were feeling was all right.

'OK. I need you to be careful, Dr Young, because I care about you. Very deeply.' It was on the tip of her tongue to keep confessing, to let him know that she was pretty sure she was in love with him, but she was also scared that such a confession would scare him off for ever and she desperately didn't want that.

Nathan's eyes had flicked down to her lips as she'd spoken and as he watched them form the words he wanted to hear, his heart grew in confidence. She cared about him. That was good. That was a start. It kept alive the hope he'd started to feel a few days ago.

Her words were good, like a lifeline, and he grabbed hold with both hands. With her words he felt the guilt, the weight he'd been lugging around for the past decade, begin to crack, begin to have pieces break off and fall away.

'I want to kiss you again, Morena,' he confessed.

'But?'

'But if I start, I don't know if I'll be able to stop.'

Warmth flooded her and for a moment she couldn't speak. 'That's quite a confession,' she finally managed to get out. It spoke of the extent of his feelings and she knew that couldn't have been easy for him. 'How about if I kiss you?'

He smiled at her attempt to lighten the moment. 'I doubt I'd be able to stop then either.'

'Then how about a kiss on the cheek? Think we can handle that?'

He pondered that then nodded. 'We need to take this thing between us slowly.' He took her hand in his and tugged her closer, kissing her cheek. As he did so she breathed him in, knowing she would take this moment with her to dreamland.

'I'll see you tomorrow at the hospital,' he said after drawing back.

'OK.' She smiled at him with love in her eyes. 'Be safe.'

'I will.' Nathan squeezed her hand then waited for her to step back before bringing the bike's engine to life. He forced himself to concentrate and arrived back at his apartment uneventfully. As he garaged his bike and went inside, he couldn't help but reflect on the evening he'd just shared with Morena.

The woman was amazing, so beautiful and intelligent and everything that drew him in. It was true that he'd wanted to run a mile when he'd first realised he was attracted to her and although he'd been mildly interested in other women over the years, he'd always been able to hold himself in check. When that control had started to slip with Morena, when they'd been able to laugh and tease and even flirt with each other with such ease and familiarity, he'd begun to worry.

Thoughts of Lila had plagued him during his long and lonely nights. He'd promised to love and cherish her for ever and where he'd always carried the guilt of her death, it was compounded by the extra guilt of desiring another woman when he should be holding onto his wife's memory.

Discovering that Morena was a single mother, that she had a young baby, had been just what he'd needed to pull right back, knowing it would be impossible for the mounting attraction he felt towards his colleague to continue.

He'd been responsible for his wife's death, been responsible for the death of his unborn son, and that wasn't something a man simply pushed aside and forgot. He was to blame and nothing that happened between himself and Morena would ever let him forget that.

Shrugging off his jacket and going through to the bathroom, Nathan prepared for bed. When he was lying there, the ceiling fan whirring gently to stir up a breeze on the hot summer night, his thoughts began to race, as they had every night since he'd first met Morena.

Usually, when he thought about her, visions of Lila would intrude and he'd be swamped once more. First a vision of his pretty wife laughing at him, of the radiance in her face, which had always managed to make him feel as though he were the luckiest man alive. Then those visions would change to one of her lying on the floor where he'd found her, her eyes open and her skin beginning to pale.

Tonight, however, that didn't happen. Tonight when he lay there and started to think about Morena, how amazing it had felt to hold her, to dance with her, to see how much she cared about him…when he thought about that, his body began to relax, his breathing evened out and he closed his eyes, reliving every little touch, every curve, every taste of her.

Tonight, the feeling of holding Connor in his arms, of

being able to stop the baby's cries, of being able to kiss his little head, stroke his soft cheek…it had been fantastic, brilliant, magnificent. Between Morena and her son, Nathan was beginning to feel not only the hope they brought but was allowing himself to want it. The guilt was starting to erode all on its own, and he knew he'd been holding it too close for too long. Morena was helping him to let go.

Tonight, for the first time in over a decade, he slept peacefully.

On Sunday, Morena and Nathan spent the day exchanging goofy looks and smiles, which was exciting in itself. It was a strange courting ritual and one she'd never been through before. Bruce had met her at a medical convention and pursued her with a relentlessness she'd often wondered about. She'd known she was nothing special to look at but she'd been swept off her feet in a whirlwind of romance, Bruce taking her to the most expensive restaurants, giving her little presents. The weeks before he'd proposed had been textbook romance.

But this…these little glances, little touches, little snatches of moments by themselves…it was powerful, thrilling and erotic. Love seemed to well up so much within her heart she was positive it was going to spill over.

She might not know what his favourite colour was, what his mother's name was or even when his birthday was. Those little things were inconsequential because she knew how to tease him, how to make him smile, how to make those chocolaty brown eyes of his smoulder with desire—desire for *her*.

Both Kaylee and Ivan were released into Mr Dinsmore's care and the reports about Simon were that he was out of ICU and could easily be transferred back to Victor Harbor Hospital to be closer to his family. Morena was very glad for her friend and that things had turned out the way they had.

That night, Nathan dined with Morena again after an uneventful hospital shift and Morena couldn't help watching the way he was with Connor. Now that the walls had started coming down, his inhibitions were almost gone. Nathan would voluntarily pick the baby up, cradling and cooing to him. Unfortunately, Connor was still out of sorts and Morena idly wondered whether her son was instinctively picking up on the change in his life, having another adult around.

'How did he sleep last night?' Nathan asked as he stirred the pasta on the stove.

'Not well. He woke up not long after you left and I was up pacing the floor with him for at least two hours.'

Nathan crossed to her side and put one hand on her shoulder and the other on Connor's head, automatically feeling his forehead. 'You should have said something earlier. Hmm, he's a little warm.'

'Well, we have had a week of stinking hot weather. I've been keeping his fluids up, Mum's been making sure he's cool at her house, but even she said he's been out of sorts.'

'Is it us?' Nathan looked into her eyes and saw she knew exactly what he meant.

'I'm not sure. It might be, but he likes you being here. Last night he was looking around the room and I wondered whether he was looking for you.'

'Really?'

'Yes.'

'Mother's intuition?'

She smiled at that and shrugged. 'Or maybe it's just that I want you here,' she said softly.

Nathan's only reply was to nod and drop a kiss to her

forehead, before returning to the stove to check the pasta sauce. Connor continued to grizzle.

'I'll make him a bottle and see if that helps.' Nathan took Connor from her and, true enough, the grizzling stopped a little but not much.

'You're not going to feed him?'

'He doesn't want me. He much prefers the bottle.'

'When did that happen?'

'This morning. It's like he's just switched off the mummy switch. I keep trying him but with no success.' Morena found it difficult to keep the disappointment out of her voice but knew she'd failed when Nathan put his arm around her.

'It's OK. You can't feed him for ever.'

'I know that, it's just…it was a special time for us, just me and Connor, and now it's over. I knew it would happen, expected it, but I also thought I'd have to wean him off slowly, but he seems to have made that decision without me. I miss it already and it's only been a day.'

Connor started to grizzle again and Morena shook the prepared bottle and went to sit down with him. Even with the bottle, though, he didn't settle. She checked his nappy— it was fine.

'Perhaps he's teething?' Nathan offered.

'I've given him some teething gel.' She sighed and held her son on her knee. 'What's wrong, darling? Tell Mummy.' Connor's answer was to cry louder.

'Let me try him with the bottle,' Nathan suggested, and Morena handed both her son and the bottle over. To her astonishment, Connor settled in Nathan's big and powerful arms and began to drink his bottle.

'Great.' She threw her arms up in the air. 'It's *me* he doesn't want.' Tears started to prick behind her lids and she turned away.

'It's not that, Morena.'

'I know. I know. I'm just being over-emotional.' She went into the kitchen and checked the dinner. 'At least we know he's not out of sorts because of your presence.'

'True.'

Morena turned the burners down low so their dinner didn't spoil. Connor finished his bottle and then, thankfully, was more than willing to be returned to his mother. She cuddled him gently and soon he was asleep. They managed to eat dinner in peace but the moment they'd finished, Connor woke up, startling Morena with his ear-splitting cry.

'Something's wrong,' she said, totally alert, her mind racing to try and figure it out.

'What?'

'I don't know. It just is. This isn't right. He hasn't been right all week long.'

'Have you given him a check-up?' Nathan followed her into Connor's room, as tense and as worried as Morena herself. He bent and kissed the baby's head after his mother had picked him up. 'He's burning up. Where do you keep the children's paracetamol?'

Morena pointed to the bottle up high on the top cupboard shelf. Connor was crying and coughing and in the next instant had been sick.

'Where's your medical bag?'

'At the clinic,' Morena said.

'It might be his ears.' Nathan picked up the lamp from the dresser and directed the light around Connor's ears. The baby cried harder and squirmed. 'Hard to tell. I need an otoscope. If it is his ears, paracetamol won't be strong enough.'

'I checked his ears a few weeks ago and although they were a little red, they soon settled. What do I do now?' she asked, concern and worry clouding her logical thought processes.

'Let's get him to the hospital.'

Morena nodded and together they packed everything up and hurried out to her car. After Morena had put Connor into his car seat, she realised she was shaking too much to drive.

'Here you go,' she said, handing her keys over. Nathan took them without a word and slid behind the wheel, adjusting the seat for his longer frame. Morena settled herself in the back seat, next to Connor, holding his hand as she closed her eyes, praying that her son was all right.

She was a doctor, for crying out loud. She saw young babies all day long, was able to diagnose and treat them, and yet when it came to her own son she was a mess. Had she overlooked something important? Was it going to be a simple diagnosis of earache or was it something worse which she couldn't have foreseen? Had she been so caught up in her own life, spending time with Nathan, listening to her own feelings, that she hadn't picked up on the signals Connor had been trying to communicate?

By the time they pulled up at the hospital Morena was only just managing to hold herself together. Her hands were shaking so badly that she couldn't get Connor's seat belt un-buckled. Nathan did it and lifted the baby out, holding him close and putting his other arm around Morena as they walked into the hospital.

Dr Jewel Book was the registrar on duty that night, a doctor Morena was more than comfortable with when it came to dealing with her son.

'I don't believe we've met,' Jewel said to Nathan, as she walked across the small examination room to get her otoscope. 'I've heard all about you, but it's nice to meet you at last, Nathan.'

Nathan nodded politely but his focus was on Morena and Connor. He wanted to be there for her, to offer his support, his comfort, his love. He wanted to make sure nothing hurt either Morena or her son, and the powerful need to protect her engulfed him. It was something he hadn't felt for so long—the need to protect—and it shook him a little. The last person he'd felt the need to protect had been Lila—and he hadn't done a very good job of that.

He watched as Morena sat on the bed, holding her son still so Jewel could look in his ears. Why was the woman moving so slowly? Couldn't she see that Connor was in pain? The poor baby was still crying and Nathan felt as though his heart would break if he didn't stop soon.

Morena looked drawn and exhausted and he wanted nothing more that to take that away, to let her know she wasn't in this alone, that he was there with her, worrying about Connor, sharing the pain of parenting.

As Jewel continued to go through the motions of checking Connor out, Nathan leaned against the wall and watched, astounded at the anxiety gripping his heart. Nothing could happen to Connor. Nothing could happen to Morena. He needed them both in his life because, without realising it, without having any clue how it had happened, they'd become vitally important to him.

He loved them. He loved them both and he wanted them both…with him. For ever!

CHAPTER TEN

AN HOUR later, Nathan pulled Morena's car up outside her house and waited for her to get Connor out before he garaged the car. He sat there for a moment, reliving the flashes of memory from the past. Being called to the hospital, the waiting, the smells, the faceless people passing by while he sat in the small waiting room reserved for those who were there to see their loved ones one last time.

The anxiety, the tension, the fear, the paranoia. All of it had been there that fateful day and it had been there tonight. He had to remind himself that Connor and Morena were both fine, they were alive and there was nothing more wrong with the baby other than a perforated eardrum. They'd picked up some antibiotics and Connor had already swallowed his first dose. Both he and Morena knew that within twenty-four hours the baby would be far more settled than he'd been all week. Everyone was good. Everyone was alive. Everyone was fine.

And he loved them…and that was not fine.

He thought back to Morena's acronym for finally, I'm not emotional. Was that what he was trying to achieve with his life? To find emotional stability or to run from it? Was that what he'd been doing for the past ten years? Emotionally distancing himself from everyone, living off the guilt which had never seemed to diminish? At least it hadn't…until he'd met Morena.

Instead of thinking about the past, he now preferred to spend the time with Morena and Connor—time he couldn't stop himself from craving. Hope had flared brightly, the hope that he could take the step to move on with his life, to finally put Lila and her tragic death behind him, to allow himself to breathe once more.

But falling in love?

He loved Morena. That much was glaringly obvious and he couldn't believe how bad it made him feel for Lila. He'd loved Lila. He'd married Lila and they'd been starting their life together, and then…

Nathan locked the car and strode towards Morena's apartment. She hadn't had it easy in the past either and he wasn't ignorant of that fact, but he wasn't quite sure what to do next.

She was still settling Connor down in his room so Nathan set about tidying up and he'd just finished the dishes when she came out.

'Asleep?' he asked as he wiped his hands dry.

'Yes. Finally.' She shook her head. 'I can't believe I was so blind to my own child's symptoms. I can't believe I was so useless at the hospital.'

'You were there as a mother, not a doctor, Morena. No one will think anything of it.'

She scoffed. 'You don't know half of the people in this town but thank you for saying so anyway.' Morena walked over to give him a hug but he took her hands and held her at arm's length. 'What's wrong?' she asked innocently, but felt a prickling of apprehension as Nathan looked down at her, his dark eyes filled with anguish.

'I need to go.'

'Oh.' She couldn't hide her disappointment. 'But that's not all. Right?'

He nodded. He should have known he couldn't pretend, not with her. 'I think…' He looked down at her hands, which he still held in his, hoping against hope that he didn't hurt her too much, that she hadn't already given him her heart. He shrugged. 'I just need to think.'

Morena was silent, wondering if that was all or if there was more.

'It's just that…' Nathan dropped her hands and turned from her, walking from the kitchen into the lounge room. 'I'm mixed up. All right? I can't help the way I feel. I just need…time.'

'That's fine.'

'No. Don't be understanding. I don't know how much time I'll need, Morena. It could be days, weeks, months—years?'

'You're running. Why are you running? Is it because of what happened tonight? With Connor?' She didn't wait for him to answer. 'I know you're uncomfortable around babies but I'd sort of hoped that you'd broken through that.'

'I had—or, at least, I thought I had.' He pointed towards Connor's room. 'I love that little guy. I really do, Morena.'

'Ah. And because of that, you need distance.' Realisation flooded her face. Did that mean he also had stronger feelings for her? Dared she even begin to consider the possibility that he loved her? Was that what was freaking him out? Making him withdraw? She wasn't game enough to voice her concerns in case it made him run from her completely. She'd found it a little unnerving just how well he knew her, so he would find it probably more so if he realised she'd been able to read his emotions so easily.

'Yes.' Nathan swallowed over the dryness of his throat. Did she know him *that* well? Could she see that he loved her? He didn't want her to see that because if he failed her the way he'd failed Lila… He closed his eyes. He couldn't think about that now. 'I need to go.'

He spun on his heel and headed for the door, amazed when she didn't try to stop him. She followed him but stood on the threshold as he crossed it.

'I'm glad you didn't ride your bike here,' was all she said, and it was the most perfect thing as far as he was concerned. It showed him right there and then just how much she *did* care for him, that even when he was trying to break things off with her, to try and give himself more space, all she was concerned about was his safety. She was right, too. He doubted he'd even have been able to hold his bike up, given the state he was in.

Nathan stood on the footpath outside her apartment and looked at her, a vision of loveliness silhouetted in the doorway. Then he turned and walked away.

He was doing the right thing…wasn't he?

'So what's actually going on between the two of you?' Sally asked the next afternoon as Morena sat at her desk, writing up notes.

Morena looked up at her friend. 'I don't know.'

'Well—do you love him?'

Morena frowned and indicated that her friend should shut the door. Sally did so and settled down in the chair opposite for a good chat. 'Well? You can tell me the truth. Nathan's off for the afternoon, remember?'

'Of course I'm in love with him. I wouldn't be so miserable if I wasn't.'

'Yay!' Sally clapped her hands and quickly got up, rushing around the desk to hug Morena. 'That's the best news.'

'Really? Doesn't feel like it.' Morena put her pen down and sighed. 'I love the man but I'm totally confused.'

'What's happened?'

'He said he needs time. He's been through a lot, Sally.'

'Such as?'

'I'm not really at liberty to discuss it.'

Sally growled. 'Oh, you doctors! You're so good at keeping secrets. Well, you do know what's wrong with him?'

'I do.'

'And? Why aren't you fixing it?'

'Because he's asked for time, Sally. Didn't you hear me?'

'Look. You love him and if he wants time it means he's confused. No man in his right mind is able to wander through the wilderness without getting lost. He needs to be guided, to be shown the way. Stick a big ring through his nose if you have to and get him out of there. He's a brilliant doctor, Morena, and he fits so perfectly into this practice—into your life.' Sally's voice was caring and tender. 'I wondered whether you'd ever get over Bruce. Not necessarily over being in love because I think he killed that well and truly when he cheated on you, but rather getting over the way he mentally abused you. You've come through that, you've grown, you've triumphed. That's *incredible*, Morena. And now you've been shown what real love is like. Been given the opportunity to find true happiness. You've come through the rough weather and it's clear skies ahead. Getting over someone putting you down in every area of your life is amazing. That's a huge thing to come to terms with, but somehow you have.' She paused. 'You *have*, haven't you?'

'I have,' Morena confirmed. 'Nathan helped me to see that. He showed me that Bruce was incredibly shallow and perhaps I was, too, back then, but having Connor has changed me and Nathan made me realise that, even if he did it indirectly. Having someone who listens when you talk as though you're the most intelligent woman on the planet…having someone who only has to look at you with such a smouldering, sexy gaze to have you going up in flames…having someone—Nathan—hold me as though I'm the most important person in the world…' Both women sighed with longing.

'Then why on earth are you sitting around here? Go and talk to him. Help him out, guide him. If you don't he'll flounder and the only area of his life that will bring him happiness will be his professional life.' The penny dropped with Sally. 'Oh. *That's* why he moves around every six months. He's running from his past.'

'You're no dummy,' was all Morena said. 'Thanks. I've heard what you've said and I'll think about it. I just don't want to push him too far, too fast because he might take off for good.'

'He needs you. You two are perfect for each other.'

'Thanks for the vote of confidence.'

Morena did think about what her friend had said. She *had* been given a second chance with Nathan…or was it a *real* chance as she and Bruce had been a wrong fit right from the start? That wasn't at all how it was with Nathan. From their earliest acquaintance she'd felt as though her heart had known his for ever. That sort of feeling, that sort of *love* didn't come along every day, and the fact that she hadn't even been looking was a miracle in itself.

She decided that she would try and speak to him that night. The sooner, the better. She knew he was hurting, trying to sort out his past. He'd been swimming in guilt for so long he was having trouble trying to get past it.

If only he'd let her help…

With her resolve firmly in place, Morena focused and finished her work, called her mother to say she might be a bit late picking up Connor and crossed to the mirror to check her hair and make-up.

'Ugh!' She started to pull her hair from its messy ponytail to try to get it into some sort of order.

'I don't think so.' Nathan's deep voice came from her doorway and she spun around to look at him. She hadn't heard him there, hadn't realised her door had been slightly ajar and hadn't realised how much she'd missed him that afternoon.

The moment stretched on and although she knew she needed to say something, her mind was blank—filled only with thoughts of him, concerns for him, love for him. What had she been doing? She'd been checking her appearance. That was right.

She lowered her hands to her sides, her hair falling loosely around her shoulders and framing her face. 'I'm a mess,' she finally said, not at all surprised that her voice was a breathless whisper. He was standing there, looking at her, drinking her in as though he was a man who'd crawled through the hot, dry desert and she was his oasis.

'No.' Nathan slowly shook his head but didn't come into the room. 'You're…' he breathed out '…stunning.' This was the first time he'd seen her hair loose and it was as though he'd been knocked for a six. The strawberry blonde strands framed her face, the ends curling slightly as they bounced just past her shoulders. Her blue eyes were brightened by the pale pink top she wore and the knee-length skirt accentuated her incredible legs.

'Nathan?'

He could hear the imploring, the confusion, the pain in her voice and he hated himself for being responsible for it. He loved her. It was crazy but he did. He'd tried to ignore the emotion but the more he did, the stronger it became, and now here she was, standing before him. The clinic was finished for the day. Sally had gone home. There was no one here but the two of them—the two of them looking at each other as though nothing else mattered in the world. Could he really let go of the past and start a future with her?

Morena swallowed the fear she was experiencing. How on earth was she supposed to reach him? Was she going to lose him? Lose him for ever? 'Why did you come back?' she asked.

'Pardon?'

'You're here. At the clinic. You're supposed to be enjoying your time off, not coming to work when everyone's gone home.'

'True.' He cleared his throat. 'Well, I uh…wanted to talk to you.'

That was a good sign…wasn't it? Morena's heart was pounding wildly in her chest and she wasn't sure whether Nathan was about to say he either didn't want to have anything to do with her or whether he was ready to profess his feelings.

'What about?' Her voice broke on a squeak and she closed her eyes, willing herself to be calm about this.

'About us.'

'Us?'

'Yes. I've asked you this question before, Morena, but I need to ask you again. How do you feel about me?'

Morena couldn't breathe. Her heart was swelling with love, fear and uncertainty, but when she looked into his eyes she saw the same emotions mirrored there. 'I love you, Nathan.'

He didn't move. Didn't nod, didn't smile. He just stood there. 'Do you think that's wise?'

'Wise or not, it's how I feel. I love you and I always will. It doesn't matter what does or doesn't happen between us— my love is yours for ever and if you decide you don't want me…' Her voice broke but she cleared her throat and forced herself to go on. 'If you don't want me then I'll deal with that.'

'What if I hurt you? What if I mess up again and you or Connor get hurt?'

'You'll hurt us more if you leave us.' His words, his attitude were giving her hope, hope that he was almost there, almost had two feet into the future, and she realised he did need a shove. 'I'm also a doctor, Nathan. I fix people's hurts. It's what I do.'

'You can't fix *this* pain.'

'Oh, can't I?' Determination ripped through her and she came around her desk, striding purposely towards him. When she was toe to toe with him she reached up, laced her fingers into his hair and urged his head down so his lips could meet hers. She poured all her passion, frustration and intense love into the kiss to let him know there was *nothing* about this relationship she wasn't going to fight for.

It only took a split second for Nathan to capitulate and gather Morena into his arms, to drink from the well of love she was so generously offering. It was only then he realised just how much he'd missed her, just how much he needed her, just how much he loved her.

'We belong together,' she panted against his mouth as she went back for more of what they both wanted so much.

Eventually it was Nathan, the war still fighting within him, who put her from him…but not too far. 'I…I'm still confused and you shouldn't be in the middle of that, but I can't help it. I need you.'

'I'm here. I love you. I want to help you.'

'You *can't* help me!' The pain, the anger, the frustration—they were all there in his voice.

'Why not?'

'Because I feel as though I'm cheating on my wife,' he blurted out, and turned away from her. 'I can't help it. I feel like I'm cheating on Lila because I lie awake at night, yearning for your touch.' He looked over his shoulder at her, his eyes intense. 'I burn for you, Morena, and that just swamps me with more guilt. Guilt about Lila.'

'She died, Nathan. Over ten years ago. She died and it's

only natural that a part of you died with her.' She reached out to touch his shoulder and forced him to look at her. 'You were married to her so it's natural you feel that way.'

'I promised to love her. To honour her. To cherish her. In sickness and in health and…and then I…I wasn't even there when she died.'

And that was the crux of it all. 'Where were you?' Morena's voice was gentle, encouraging.

'I was late getting home.'

'Why?'

'Because I'd stopped off at the uni bar to have a drink with friends.' He looked past her, seeing into the days that were long gone but were still obviously very fresh in his mind. 'We'd just finished an exam—one of the big ones—and I'd called Lila to let her know I'd be a bit late. She said that was OK but that she wasn't feeling too good. I told her I'd only stay for one drink and then I'd be home.' He shook his head sadly. 'If I'd just gone straight home…'

'How did she die?'

'Aneurysm.'

'Where?'

'In her brain.'

'Oh, Nathan.' Morena reached for him and he went willingly into her arms. 'What could you have done? If you'd been there?'

'Nothing.' He shook his head for emphasis. 'But at least she wouldn't have had to die alone.'

'It would have been quick.'

'That's what they told me. It was just one of those freak things that happen from time to time.'

'Nathan.' Morena kissed him, wanting her love for him to help him through this pain.

'I should have been there.'

'But you weren't. You can't change the past, neither can you hide from your future.'

'I'm not…' He stopped for as he said the words he realised that was exactly what he was doing.

'You haven't been grieving for Lila all these years, you've been saturating yourself with guilt, and that's not healthy. Guilt brings with it so many other emotions—doubt and fear, as well as constantly questioning yourself. You've created a prison for yourself but you don't realise that you also hold the key.'

Nathan looked down at her, a faint ray of hope in his eyes. 'How?'

'Remove the bars.'

'How?'

'Forgive yourself.'

'But I can't forget what hap—'

'No one's asking you to forget. No one's asking you to discount the life you had with Lila, but *your* life has moved on. Till death us do part. Those were the vows you took and you can honour them. *You've* moved on both physically and mentally. You keep changing jobs, keep working in different practices so you don't have to connect with people, so you can live in your guilt.' Morena shook her head. 'That time is over. You've not only conquered your prejudice against pregnant women and young babies, you've outgrown your guilt.'

'I want to believe you.'

'All right, then.' She stepped back and held his hands. 'Look at me. Tell me what you see.'

Nathan's gaze slid over her, drinking her in. 'I see a woman who has overcome a lot of personal pain.' Morena nodded, trying to encourage him. 'I see a woman who's a wonderful, caring and loving mother. I see a woman who sets me on fire every time I look at her.'

She gasped at his words but nodded once more, indicating he should continue.

'I see a woman who won't give up on me, who loves me.'

'I do.'

'I see a woman who feels perfect in my arms, feels perfect in my life.'

Morena's breathing started to increase and she sighed with longing as he reached out and gently caressed her cheek, she leaned into his touch.

'I see the woman I love.'

'Oh, Nathan.' She couldn't take it any longer and neither could he, both desperate to feel each other's bodies as close as possible.

'Forgive yourself,' she whispered in his ear a few minutes later as he held her. 'Don't forget the past because it makes us into who we are. You showed me that. You made me realise that I'm not the same woman I was when I married Bruce. I'm different. Stronger. Confident. You helped me understand that. You helped me understand that I would be foolish not to take a step into the unknown, into the possible void of love, but thankfully I've stepped onto solid ground.'

'It is solid. My love for you is very solid, Morena. For you and Connor. I love that little guy so much and I've missed him today almost as much as I've missed you.'

'He's missed you as well.'

Nathan closed his eyes and held her close. 'I'm sorry.'

'No. Don't be. How can you be sorry when we're together, when we've worked our way through such a difficult time?'

'It shows us we have the strength to move forward. You give me strength.'

'I do?'

'Yes. I hadn't realised just how much.'

'Nathan…why did you walk away? After we'd returned

from the hospital with Connor? Was it just because you were feeling guilty about Lila?'

'Why do you ask?'

'Because it felt as though there was more, but I'm not sure what.'

Nathan nodded. 'It's because I'd realised I loved you. You and Connor. That I'd moved on. Yes, I felt guilty but there was also the complete and utter fear that if I loved you, if I admitted it to myself and let myself believe it, I was putting myself at risk once more. If anything happens to either you or Connor…I don't know if I'll survive.'

'I know. I know.' She kissed him. 'I know. That's how I feel, but we can't live our lives being swamped by fear.'

'Fear is the thing you fear the most?'

'Exactly. It's no way to live and I want to live, Nathan.'

'I want that, too. I want to be with you, with Connor. I want us be together. For ever.'

'We will.'

'I'm asking you to marry me, Morena.' Nathan looked into her eyes, only the slightest hesitation and concern left.

'I know,' she responded. 'And I'm saying yes.'

'Really?'

Morena laughed. 'You'd better believe it, mate. You're stuck with me. Me and Connor. For ever.'

Nathan joined in her laughter. 'I couldn't be happier.'

MILLS & BOON

MEDICAL™
On sale 7th March 2008

THE SURGEON'S FATHERHOOD SURPRISE
by Jennifer Taylor

BRIDES OF PENHALLY BAY
*Bachelor doctors become husbands and fathers –
in a place where hearts are made whole*

Surgeon Jack Tremayne lives the VIP life – until his world is turned upside down when he learns he is the father of a three-year-old boy… Jack returns to his home town of Penhally Bay with little Freddie, where he soon finds his life inextricably entangled with that of nurse and single mum Alison Myers.

THE ITALIAN SURGEON CLAIMS HIS BRIDE
by Alison Roberts

Esteemed Italian surgeon Paolo Romano's toddler needs a nanny, and nurse Jenna desperately needs a job. Jenna knows the position is only temporary; however, the chemistry between Jenna and the charming Paolo is electrifying from the moment they meet…

DESERT DOCTOR, SECRET SHEIKH
by Meredith Webber

Dr Jenny Stapleton devotes herself to those in need around the globe, risking her life but never her heart. Then she meets Dr Kam Rahman…who is actually Sheikh Kamid Rahman. Kam is soon to ascend the throne – and he wants this desert doctor as his queen!

MILLS & BOON®

MEDICAL™

proudly presents

Brides of Penhally Bay

Featuring Dr Nick Tremayne

*A pulse-raising collection of emotional, tempting romances and
heart-warming stories — devoted doctors, single fathers,
Mediterranean heroes, a sheikh and his guarded heart,
royal scandals and miracle babies…*

THE SURGEON'S FATHERHOOD SURPRISE
Jennifer Taylor

Brides of Penhally Bay

MEDICAL

Book Four

THE SURGEON'S FATHERHOOD SURPRISE

by Jennifer Taylor

on sale 7th March 2008

A COLLECTION TO TREASURE FOREVER!
One book available every month

Celebrate 100 years of pure reading pleasure with Mills & Boon®

To mark our centenary, each month we're publishing a special 100th Birthday Edition. These celebratory editions are packed with extra features and include a FREE bonus story.

Now that's worth celebrating!

4th January 2008

The Vanishing Viscountess by Diane Gaston
With FREE story The Mysterious Miss M
This award-winning tale of the Regency Underworld launched Diane Gaston's writing career.

1st February 2008

Cattle Rancher, Secret Son by Margaret Way
With FREE story His Heiress Wife
Margaret Way excels at rugged Outback heroes…

15th February 2008

Raintree: Inferno by Linda Howard
With FREE story Loving Evangeline
A double dose of Linda Howard's heady mix of passion and adventure.

Don't miss out! From February you'll have the chance to enter our fabulous monthly prize draw. See special 100th Birthday Editions for details.

www.millsandboon.co.uk

FREE

4 BOOKS AND A SURPRISE GIFT!

We would like to take this opportunity to thank you for reading this Mills & Boon® book by offering you the chance to take FOUR more specially selected titles from the Medical™ series absolutely FREE! We're also making this offer to introduce you to the benefits of the Mills & Boon® Reader Service™—

- ★ **FREE home delivery**
- ★ **FREE gifts and competitions**
- ★ **FREE monthly Newsletter**
- ★ **Books available before they're in the shops**
- ★ **Exclusive Reader Service offers**

Accepting these FREE books and gift places you under no obligation to buy; you may cancel at any time, even after receiving your free shipment. Simply complete your details below and return the entire page to the address below. You don't even need a stamp!

YES! Please send me 4 free Medical books and a surprise gift. I understand that unless you hear from me, I will receive 6 superb new titles every month for just £2.89 each, postage and packing free. I am under no obligation to purchase any books and may cancel my subscription at any time. The free books and gift will be mine to keep in any case.

M8ZEE

Ms/Mrs/Miss/Mr..Initials ....
BLOCK CAPITALS PLEASE

Surname ....

Address ....

....

....Postcode ....

Send this whole page to:
The Reader Service, FREEPOST CN81, Croydon, CR9 3WZ